D1578205

THE
ELEANOR FARJEON
BOOK

THE
ELEANOR FARJEON

BOOK

A TRIBUTE TO HER
LIFE AND WORK
1881–1965

INTRODUCTION BY
NAOMI LEWIS

ILLUSTRATED BY
EDWARD ARDIZZONE

HAMISH HAMILTON

First published in Great Britain 1966
by Hamish Hamilton Ltd,
90 Great Russell Street, London, W.C.1

Reprinted September 1966

© 1966 Hamish Hamilton Ltd
Illustrations © 1966 Edward Ardizzone

Printed in Great Britain by
Western Printing Services Ltd, Bristol

CONTENTS

		Page
Introduction NAOMI LEWIS		I
Poor Stainless MARY NORTON		II
The Italian Boy GILLIAN AVERY		28
The Gold Angel EILÍS DILLON		47
Gabble-Gabble JAMES REEVES		59
The Chief's Daughter ROSEMARY SUTCLIFF		62
The White Horse RUTH AINSWORTH		81
The Best Shoes Brogeen Ever Made PATRICIA LYNCH		94
The Frog and the Ox IAN SERRAILLIER		114
Rainbow WILLIAM MAYNE		117
The Reindeer Slippers BARBARA WILLARD		141
The Sampler DOROTHY CLEWES		159
Tea with Eleanor Farjeon RUMER GODDEN		171

INTRODUCTION

Naomi Lewis

The quest for Eleanor Farjeon lies, very fittingly, cross-country, and curious country too. Even time plays tricks. For instance she is, we would all agree, one of the true enduring names in the field of children's writing. Yet at what point did she cross into that terrain? The works which have been appearing, in the most inviting editions, through the 1950s and '60s—*The Little Bookroom, Kaleidoscope* and the rest—are quite often re-issues or new selections of tales first published in the 1920s and '30s. Yet in that period their author was much better known for her witty theatrical productions, written, with her brother Herbert Farjeon, for adults.

Again, if we try to pin down the single essential Farjeon book for the young, what will it be? Probably, *Martin Pippin in the Apple Orchard*.

Yet that unique, puzzling, magical book, first published in 1921 but set down earlier than that, was not intended for children at all. It was "written and posted, tale by tale, to a Sussex-loving friend in the trenches". That it came to be regarded as a children's story never ceased to surprise its author. To be sure, *Martin Pippin in the Daisy Field*, which followed many years later, in 1937, *is* for, as well as about, little girls, but this was consciously done, and something of the spark of the first has gone.

Time and the mood of the day must affect the course of every writer's muse. Eleanor Farjeon was born in 1881, but the dreaming, bookish, bespectacled little girl that she became, the only sister among three admired but dissimilar brothers, was more than usually late in leaving the childhood world, late too in finding herself as a writer. So it happened that the time when her gifts came to flower was at a time that favoured the strongest aspect of her imagination; the golden fantasy, the cheerful fairy-tale view of human life. She had no need to swim against the tide, and this was a situation both happy and touched with danger. Yet it is fascinating to see how many works of fantasy, as well as those from the child's view (such as A. A. Milne's *When We Were Very Young*), were written for adult readers in the first twenty or thirty years of this century. Many of them are current still: *The Crock of Gold, The Man Who Was Thursday,*

Lolly Willowes, Orlando, Lady into Fox, the stories of de la Mare—all of them crossing the supernatural frontier. It is with these, perhaps, that *Martin Pippin* originally belonged.

But something more must be noted about the days when Eleanor Farjeon first appeared as a writer. As we look back over half a century's distance to the last bright years—deceptively bright —before the First World War, we see perhaps the final surgings in England of an ancient pastoral dream—old enough even in Shakespeare's day to be charmingly mocked in the woodland glades of *As You Like It.* Yet it was to stay alive and green for many a day after that. For the countryside—an idealized harmony of man and creature and changing season—has been, from English poetry's first beginnings, its most persistent subject. Until quite lately indeed, when something of a revolution has taken place in the reading and writing of poetry in schools, children—often against all evidence— have gone on writing of a countryside of daisied fields where shepherds pipe all day, till dusk, when nightingales take over the tuneful lay: so pervasive is the power of this literary vision. And around 1912 and 1913—a time most vividly brought to life in Eleanor Farjeon's second autobiographical volume, we find a group of writers and artists attempting to link the pastoral fact with the pastoral idea. This was a period of the rural week-end cottage, the long tramps over country lanes, the clay pipes and blackthorn walking sticks, the cider, the newly discovered folk-songs—and the reflection of these things in various "Georgian" poems.

True poetry did come out of the orchard cottage and the woodland walk—and none of it better than Edward Thomas's. For Thomas, whom Eleanor knew in the four important years that held all his poetry-writing, and then his death in war—Thomas not only lived in the country but saw it plain: the back-breaking clay, the raw new house, the rain, the way in which the recurring seasons preserve and present old griefs. He caught these things in poems of rare and poignant beauty. But to Eleanor Farjeon, trudging over the same clay fields, disenchantment never came. Summer pervades her books: milkmaids, pedlars, elves and shepherd boys people her countryside. Moreover, the pages are lit by a kind of ecstasy, a mood first known in her childish fairy-tale reading and day-dream journeys, later in heightened yet dream-like moments of life itself; it remains the essential element in her work. Of this she was to write:

Ecstasy cannot be constant, or it would kill. The glow comes and fades, comes and fades. . . . Writing gets done in queer irregular ways at queer irregular times. I still want everything so much, I don't know where to choose. If I had had a regular disciplined education, should I have learnt how and what to choose? . . . Would it have stopped the glow from coming so often, and dimmed it when it did come? I don't know. I have no rule to go by. It seems to me that there are no rules, only instances. . . .

Rule or not, she has left a number of clues to the roots, at least, of the Farjeon gift; and for these we must turn for a start to what many may think the greatest of all her books, *A Nursery in the Nineties.* Here, in most striking re-animation, she traces the life of a boy who would be in time her father, now —in 1854—in the gold-fields of Australia, now an editor and novelist and friend of Dickens; she traces too the story of her mother, the daughter of the American actor Joseph Jefferson; she writes of the warm, devoted turbulent London home, always filled with lively literary and theatrical figures, and in which the four young Farjeons led their own intense and close-knit lives.

Eleanor, short-sighted and shy, had no formal schooling; on the other hand she did have an encouraging writer father (the severer disciplines came from the brothers' side) and the free range of an enormous jumble of books. "I never learnt how to learn," she later reflected.

No wonder that when I came to write books myself, they were a muddle of fiction and fact, fantasy and truth. I have never quite succeeded in distinguishing one from the other. . . . Seven maids with seven brooms, sweeping for half a hundred years, have never managed to clear my mind of its dust of vanished temples and flowers and kings, the curls of ladies, the sighing of poets, the laughter of lads and girls: those golden ones, who, like chimney sweepers, must all come to dust in some little bookroom or other—and sometimes, by luck, come again for a moment to light.

But the strongest influence on her mind, she reveals, was a game called TAR—initial abbreviations of the names Tessie and Ralph, two daydream characters with whom she and her brother Harry, with all the force of their strong imaginations, identified themselves.

Tar was the usual child's game of pretending to be someone else; but I think in our case it was extended to a degree of intensity, complexity and accomplishment never equalled. The game began when I was about five years old, and for more than twenty years it continued to be the chief experience of my inward and outward life. . . . At an age, and long past it, when life's horizons should have been widening, they kept their narrow circle, while those of TAR widened increasingly. I had no desire for new adventures, friends, experience outside this powerful game.

"In our case . . . never equalled." At the time when Eleanor Farjeon wrote this important passage (that is, in the early 1930s) the research on the Brontë children had not yet reached the stage of publication. Would a harder scene, a harder literary climate, such as the Brontës knew, have given her work more astringency? The Brontës were not brought up on fairy tales; their alchemy made wild romance from the seeming sawdust of political newspapers, and even (how else did those maps arise?) geographical textbooks.

One can never answer such questions. Eleanor had not, for one thing, the desperate Brontë temperament. . . . There were no imagined nymphs on the Bronte moors, nor was summer their climate. But the practice of TAR did give her, as it gave that family of genius, "the power to put in motion given persons within given scenes, and see what came of it, and . . . the flow of ease that makes writing a delight".

This writing then—not always directed at children though often about them—how does it seem today? Re-reading (for remembered impression is not enough) I, for one, am struck by the inspired craftsmanship of her stories. I would place these above her plays—though she enjoyed writing dialogue, had abundant humour and wit, and understood well the workings of the theatre. I would place them also above her verse, for though she wrote many enchanting poems that will always please sensitive children, her facility was not always her friend. Perhaps, too, she idealized the young too much in her rhymes; this tends to make readers uncomfortable. The best of her poetry possibly lay in her prose which—though she claimed to know no rules—had something of the inner tensions, the design and swift moves of poetry.

Her favourite medium (most notably seen in the Martin Pippin books) was a framework in which a number of shorter tales could be told. Chaucer used this of course; so did Boccaccio. It serves Eleanor admirably; at the same time, the separate short tales stand perfectly well on their own. *The Little Bookroom* was her own admirable selection of such stories.

How skilfully they are told! How dazzlingly each one reveals its point, yet with a seeming casual lightness. How many achieve, in their kind, an entire perfection of form and content. (I would name among these *The Kings and the Corn, The Barrel Organ, The Times, Old Surly and the Boy, Young Kate, Westwoods, The Clumber Pup.*) And though they do not deal with adult themes from an adult view, they are informed by the shrewd and ageless wisdom of the folk-tale view. Even her occasional allegory has no indigestible sediment of earnestness. Perhaps she *was* too much on the side of the prettiest goosegirl, the one with the longest, yellowest hair: one can have no other complaint.

But read above all that outstanding book *A Nursery in the Nineties*. It may be the title that has kept it from being more widely known, for it deals with a longer time, and with older people than either "nineties" or "nursery" would suggest. Adults generally come to it by chance, find themselves engrossed in its pages, report their discovery on all sides, but part from the volume grudgingly if at all. *Edward Thomas: the Last Four Years* continues Eleanor's story; the third volume—alas, left uncompleted—was to centre on her brother Herbert. Perhaps we shall see some chapters in print.

It is typical of Eleanor Farjeon that the author never was the main figure of her autobiography. She never did see herself as the centre of the picture; indeed, it is hard to think of a writer so completely, so disconcertingly lacking in vanity. "Unlike most of us, she was not ashamed of showing her feelings", as Miss Rumer Godden writes in her memorable essay. With most of us, memory touches up the picture a little. Eleanor's faithfully ruthless memory was matched by her readiness to communicate all that she recalled.

Readers in search of more of Eleanor's works still have fragments to find—not least the remarkable narrative essays she wrote introducing a selection of Frost's poems published last year (1964) and a selection of Edward Thomas's, her own choice, that has recently followed it.

Eleanor Farjeon lived to be eighty-four, but her gifts did not decline, nor did her vision change. For her, in youth, the summer was brighter, the winters more delicately beautiful than they seemed to duller imaginations; and so through her life they remained. The writing of her latest days—the autobiographical essays, an occasional story such as the last one of all called *Mr. Garden*, show a touch as sure as in any work that she wrote when she was young. Why should this not be so? Her writing at all times was absolutely an extension of herself in words, on the page. Do not think that this is true of everybody! And because of this shining immediacy, each one of us who reads is her friend and her guest, taking tea in the room at the top of those stairs (described in this book by Miss Rumer Godden) in the house that was once a stable—a house that was, like herself, a marvel—a part of Oberon's rural England in the twentieth century London of our day.

POOR STAINLESS

Mary Norton

Who takes them, that thimble, that odd sock, that pair of spectacles?
We all know how little things mysteriously disappear. It has been left
to Mary Norton to uncover the secret: they don't disappear, they are
"borrowed". It is only with such lost household objects converted
ingeniously to their own use, that these tiny people, the Borrowers, eke
out their existence right under the feet of oblivious humans. Indeed, for
years Pod lived comfortably with his wife, Homily, and daughter,
Arrietty, under the kitchen floor of the big house. One day disaster struck
and they had to start life anew amid the unfamiliar dangers of the open
air. Arrietty rather enjoyed the new experience, but her mother constantly
harked back to the good old days, in the big house.

"AND NOW," said Arrietty to Homily, "tell me
what-you-used-to-do. . . ."

The phrase run together in one eager breath had

lost its meaning as words—it described an activity, a way of passing the time while engaged in monotonous tasks. They were unpicking sequins from a square of yellowed chiffon: Homily unpicked while Arrietty threaded the glimmering circles on a string of pale blue silk. It was a fine Spring day and they sat beside the grating let into the outside wall. The sunlight fell across them in criss-cross squares, and the soft air moved their hair.

"Well," said Homily, after a moment, "did I ever tell you about the time when I lit the big candle?"

"And burned a hole in the floorboards—and in the carpet upstairs? And human beings shrieked—and your father beat you with a wax matchstick? Yes, you've told me."

"It was a candle my father borrowed to melt down for dips. It shined lovely," said Homily.

"Tell me about the time when the cook upstairs upset the boiling marmalade and it all leaked down between the cracks—"

"Oh, that was dreadful," said Homily, "but we bottled it, or most of it, in acorn cups and an empty tube called morphia. But the mess, oh dear, the mess—my mother was beside herself. There was a corner of our carpet," added Homily reflectively, "which tasted sweet for months." With a work-worn hand she smoothed down the gleaming chiffon which billowed smokelike on the moving air.

"I know what," cried Arietty suddenly, "tell me about the rat!"

"Oh, not again," said Homily.

She glanced at herself in a sequin which—to her—was about the size of a hand-mirror. "I'm going very grey," she said. She polished up the sequin with a corner of her apron and stared again, patting her hair at the temples. "Did I ever tell you about Poor Stainless?"

" Who was he?" asked Arrietty.

"One of the Knife Machine boys."

"No . . ." said Arrietty, uncertainly.

"That was the first time I went upstairs. To look for Stainless." Homily, staring into the sequin, lifted her hair a little at the temples. "Oh, dear," she said, in a slightly dispirited voice.

"I like it grey," said Arrietty warmly, gently retrieving the sequin, "it suits you. What about Poor Stainless—"

"He was lost, you see. And we were all to go up and look for him. It was an order," said Homily. "Some people thought it wrong that the women should go, too, but there it was: it was an order."

" Who gave it?" asked Arrietty.

"The grandfathers, of course. It was the first time I ever saw the scullery. After that, once I knew the way, I used to sneak up there now and again but no one ever knew. Oh, dear, I shouldn't say this to you!"

"Never mind," said Arrietty.

"Poor Stainless. He was the youngest of that family. They used to live down a hole in the plaster on a level with the table where the knife machine used to stand. They did all their borrowing in the scullery. Practically vegetarians they were—carrots, turnips, watercress, celery, peas, beans—the lot. All the stuff Crampfurl, the gardener, used to bring in in baskets. Lovely complexions they had, every one of them. Especially Stainless. Stainless had cheeks like apple blossom. 'Merry little angel' my mother used to call him. All the grown-ups were mad about Stainless—he had a kind of way with them. But not with us. We didn't like him."

"Why not?" asked Arrietty, suddenly interested.

"I don't know," said Homily, "he had mean ways—well, more like teasing kind of ways; and he never got found out. He'd coax black beetles down our chute—great things with horns they were—and we'd know it was him but we couldn't prove it. And many a time he'd creep along above our floorboards, with a bent pin on a string and hook at me through a crack in our ceiling: if we had a party, he'd do it, because he was too young to be asked. But it wasn't any fun, getting hooked by Stainless—caught me by the hair, once he did. And in those days—" said Homily complacently, taking up another sequin, "my hair was my crowning glory." She stared into the sequin reflectively, then put it down with a sigh.

"Well, anyway," she went on briskly, "Stainless disappeared. What a to do!—His mother, it seemed had sent him out to borrow parsley. Eleven-fifteen in the morning it was and, by evening, he hadn't returned. And he didn't return that night.

"Now you must understand about parsley—it's a perfectly simple borrow and a quick one. Five minutes, it should have taken him: all you had to do was to walk along the knife machine table on to a ledge at the top of the wainscot, drop down (quite a small drop) on to the draining board and the parsley always stood in an old jam jar at the back of the sink—on a zinc shelf, like, with worn holes in it.

"Some said, afterwards, Stainless was too young to be sent for parsley. They blamed the parents. But there was his mother, single handed behind the knife machine getting a meal for all that family and the elder ones off borrowing with their father and, as I told you, Stainless was always out anyway directly his mother's back was turned—plaguing us and what not and whispering down the cracks: 'I see you,' he'd say—there was no privacy with Stainless until my father wall-papered our ceiling. Well, anyway," went on Homily, pausing to get her breath, "Stainless had disappeared and the next day, a lovely sunny afternoon, at three o'clock sharp—we were all to go up and look for him. It was Mrs. Driver's afternoon out, and the maids would be having their rest.

"We all had our orders: some were to look among the garden boots and the blacking brushes; others in the vegetable bins; my father and your Uncle Hendreary's father and several of the stronger men had to carry a spanner with a wooden spoon lashed across it to unscrew the trap in the drain below the sink.

"I stopped to watch this, I remember. Several of us did. Round and round they went—like Cramp-furl does with the cider-press—on the bottom of an upturned bucket under the sink. Suddenly, there was a great clatter and the screw came tumbling off and there was a rush of greasy water all over the bucket top. Oh dear, oh dear," exclaimed Homily, laughing a little but half-ashamed of doing so, "those poor men! None of their wives would have them home again until they had climbed up into the sink proper and had the tap turned on them. *Then* it was the hot tap, which was meant to be luke-warm. Oh dear, oh dear, what a to do! But still no Stainless.

"We young ones were taken home then, but it was a good four hours before the men abandoned the search. We ate our tea in silence, I remember, while our mothers sniffed and wiped their eyes. After tea, my younger brother started playing marbles with three old dried peas he had, and my mother rebuked him and said, 'Quiet now—have you no respect? Think of your father and of all those brave men Upstairs!' The way she said 'Upstairs' made your hair stand on end.

"And, yet, you know, Arrietty, I liked the scullery, what I'd seen of it—with the sunshine coming through the yard door and falling warm on that old brick floor. And the bunches of bay-leaf and dried thyme. But I did remember there had been a mousetrap under the sink and another under the boot cupboard. Not that these were dangerous —except for those who did not know—our father would roll a potato at them and then they would go click. But they'd jump a bit when they did it and that's what startled you. No, the real danger was Crampfurl, the gardener, coming in suddenly through the yard door with the vegetables for dinner; or Mrs. Driver, the cook, back from her afternoon out, to fill a kettle. And there were other maids then in the house who might take a fancy to a radish or an apple from the barrel behind the scullery door.

"Anyway, when darkness came the rescue party was called off. Our mothers made a great fuss of the men, thankful to see them back, and brought them their suppers and fetched their slippers. And no one spoke above a whisper. And we were sent to bed.

"By that time, we too felt grave. As we lay cosily under the warm covers, we could not help but think of Stainless. Poor Stainless. Perhaps he'd gone *past* the trap and down the drain of the

sink into the sewers. We knew there were borrowers
who lived in sewers and that they were dreadful
people, wild and fierce like rats. Once, my little
brother played with one and got bitten in the
arm and his shirt stolen. And he got a dreadful
rash.

"Next day, the two grandfathers called another
meeting: they were the elders, like, and always
made the decisions. One grandfather was my
father's great uncle. I forget now who the other
was . . ."

"Never mind," said Arrietty.

"Well," said Homily, "the long and short of it
was—we were all to go Upstairs, and go throughout every room. Firbank was full of borrowers, in
those days—or so it seemed—and some we never
knew. But we was to seek them out, any we could
find, and ask about Poor Stainless. A house-to-
house search they called it."

"Goodness!" gasped Arrietty.

"We was all to go," said Homily.

"Women and children, too?"

"*All*," said Homily, "except the little 'uns."

She sat still, frowning into space, her face
seemed graven by the memory. "Some said the old
men were mad," she went on, after a moment.
"But it was wonderfully organized: we were to go
in twos—two to each room. The elder ones and the
young girls for the ground floor, the younger men
and some quite young boys for the creepers."

"What creepers?"

"The creepers up the house front, of course: they had to search the bedrooms!"

"Yes, I see," said Arrietty.

"That was the only way you could get up to the first floor in those days. It was long before your father invented his hat-pin. There was no one could tackle the stairs—the height of the treads, you see, and nothing to grip on . . ."

"Yes. Go on about the creepers."

"Early dawn it was, barely light, when the young lads were lined up on the gravel, marking from below which of the windows was open. One, two, three, GO—and they was off—all the ivy and wistaria leaves shaking like a palsy! Oh, the stories they had to tell about what they found in those bedrooms but never a sign of Stainless! One poor little lad slipped on a window-sill and gripped on a cord to save himself: it was the cord of a roller blind and the roller blind went clattering up to the ceiling and there he was—hanging on a thing like a wooden acorn. He got down in the end—swung himself back and forth until he got a grip on the pelmet, then down the curtain by the bobbles. Not much fun, though, with two great human beings in night caps, snoring away on the bed.

"We women and girls took the downstairs rooms, each with a man who knew the ropes, like. We had orders to be back by tea-time, because of the little 'uns, but the men were to search on until dusk. I had my Uncle Bolty and they'd given us the morning room. And it was on that spring day, just after it became light—" Homily paused significantly, "that I first saw the Overmantels!"

"Oh," exclaimed Arrietty, "I remember—those proud kind of borrowers who lived above the chimney-piece?"

"Yes," said Homily, "them." She thought for a moment. "You never could tell how many of them there were because you always saw them doubled in the looking glass. The overmantel went right up to the ceiling, filled with shelves and twisty pillars and plush-framed photographs. You saw them always gliding about behind the cape-gooseberries, or the jars of pipe cleaners or the japanese fans. They smelled of cigars and brandy and—something else. But perhaps that was the smell of the room. Russian leather—yes, that was it. . . ."

"Go on," said Arrietty, "did they speak to you?"

"Speak to us! Did the Overmantels speak to us!" Homily gave a short laugh, then shook her head grimly as though dismissing a memory. Her cheeks had become very pink.

"But," said Arrietty, breaking the odd silence, "at least, you saw them!"

"Oh, we saw them right enough. And heard them. There were plenty of them about that morning. It was early, you see, and they knew the human beings were asleep. There they all were, gliding about, talking and laughing among themselves—and dressed up to kill for a mouse-hunt. And they saw us all right, as we stood beside the door, but would they look at us? No, not they. Not straight, that is: their eyes slid about all the time, as they laughed and talked among themselves. They looked past us and over us and under us but never quite at us. Long, long eyes they had, and funny light tinkling voices. You couldn't make out what they said.

"After a while, my Uncle Bolty stepped forward: he cleared his throat and put on his very best voice (he could do this voice, you see, that's why they chose him for the morning-room). 'Excuse and pardon me,' he said (it was lovely the way he said it) 'for troubling and disturbing you, but have you by any chance seen—' and he went on to describe Poor Stainless, lovely complexion and all.

"Not a sign of notice did he get. Those Overmantels just went on laughing and talking and putting on airs like as if they were acting on a stage. And beautiful they looked, too (you couldn't deny it) some of the women, in their long-necked Overmantel way. The early morning sunlight shining on all that looking glass lit them all up, like, to a kind of pinky gold. Lovely it was. You couldn't help but notice. . . .

"My Uncle Bolty began to look angry and his face grew very red. 'High or low, we're borrowers

all,' he said in a loud voice, 'and this little lad—'
he almost shouted it, 'was the apple of his
mother's eye!' But the Overmantels went on
talking in a silly, flustered way, laughing a little
still, and sliding their long eyes sideways.

"My Uncle Bolty suddenly lost his temper. 'All
right,' he thundered, forgetting his special voice
and going back to his country one, 'you silly
feckless lot. High you may be but remember
this—them as dwells below the kitchen floor has
solid earth to build on and we'll outlast you
yet!'

"With that he turns away, and I go after him,
crying a little—I wouldn't know for why. Knee-
high we were in the pile of the morning-room
carpet. As we passed through the doorway a
silence fell behind us. We waited in the hall and
listened for a while. It was a long, long silence."

Arrietty did not speak. She sat there lost in
thought and gazing at her mother. After a moment,
Homily sighed and said, "Somehow, I don't seem
to forget that morning, though nothing much
happened really—when you come to think of it.
Some of the others had terrible adventures,
especially them who was sent to search the bedrooms. But your Great Uncle Bolty was right.
When they closed up most of the house, after her
Ladyship's accident, the morning room wasn't used
any more. Starved out, they must have been, those
Overmantels. Or frozen out." She sighed again

and shook her head. "You can't help but feel
sorry for them. . . .

"We all stayed up that night, even us young
ones, waiting and hoping for news. The search
parties kept arriving back in ones and twos. There
was hot soup for all and some were given brandy.
Some of the mothers looked quite grey with
worry but they kept up a good front, caring for all
and sundry as they came tumbling in down the
chute. By morning, all the searchers were home.
The last to arrive were three young lads who had
got trapped in the bedrooms when the housemaids
came up at dusk to close the windows and draw the
curtains. It had come on to rain, you see. They had
to crouch inside the fender for over an hour while
two great human beings changed for dinner. It was
a lady and gentleman and, as they dressed, they
quarrelled—and it was all to do with someone
called 'Algy'. Algy this and Algy that . . . on and
on. Scorched and perspiring as these poor boys
were, they peered out through the brass curlecues of
the fender, and took careful note of everything. At
one point, the lady took off most of her hair and
hung it on a chair back. The borrowers were
astonished. At another point, the gentleman—
taking off his socks—flung them across the room
and one landed in the fireplace. The borrowers
were terrified and pulled it out of sight; it was a
woollen sock and might begin to singe; they
couldn't risk the smell."

"How did they get away?"

"Oh, that was easy enough once the room was empty, and the guests were safely at dinner. They unravelled the sock, which had a hole in the toe, and let themselves down through the bannisters on the landing. The first two got down all right. But the last, the littlest one, was hanging in air when the butler came by with a soufflé. All was well, though, the butler didn't look up, and the little one didn't let go.

"Well, that was that. The search was called off and, for us younger ones at least, life seemed to return to normal. Then one afternoon—it must have been a week later because it was a Saturday, I remember, and that was the day our mother always took a walk down the drain-pipe to have tea with the Rain-Barrells and on this particular Saturday she took our little brother with her. Yes, that was it—anyway, we two girls, my sister and I, found ourselves alone in the house. Our mother always left us jobs to do and that afternoon it was to cut up a length of black shoe-lace to make arm-bands in memory of Stainless. Everybody was making them—it was an order 'to show respect'— and we were all to put them on together in three days' time. After a while, we forgot to be sad and chattered and laughed as we sewed. It was so peaceful, you see, sitting there together and with no fear any more of black beetles.

"Suddenly my sister looked up, as though she

had heard a noise. 'What's that?' she said, and she looked kind of frightened.

"We both of us looked round the room, then I heard her let out a cry: she was staring at a knot-hole in the ceiling. Then I saw it, too—something moving in the knot-hole: it seemed to be black but it wasn't a beetle. We could neither of us speak or move: we just sat there rivetted—watching this thing come winding down towards us out of the ceiling. It was a shiny snakey sort of thing, and it had a twist or curl in it which, as it got lower, swung round in a blind kind of way and drove us shrieking into a corner. We clung together, crying and staring, until suddenly my sister said 'Hush!'. We waited, listening. 'Someone spoke,' she whispered, staring towards the ceiling. Then we heard it—a hoarse voice, rather breathy and horribly familiar. 'I can see you!' it said.

"We were furious. We called him all sorts of names. We threatened him with every kind of punishment. We implored him to take the Thing away. But all he did was to giggle a little, and keep on saying, in that silly sing-song voice: "Taste it . . . taste it . . . it's lovely!"

"Oh," breathed Arrietty, "did you dare?"

Homily frowned. "Yes. In the end. And it was lovely," she admitted grudgingly, "it was a liquorice boot-lace."

"But where had he been all that time?"

"In the village shop."

"But—" Arrietty looked incredulous, "how did he get there?"

"It was all quite simple really. Mrs. Driver had left her shopping basket on the scullery table, with a pair of shoes to be heeled. Stainless, on his way to the parsley, heard her coming, and nipped inside a shoe. Mrs. Driver put the shoes in the basket and carried them off to the village. She put down the basket on the shop counter while she gossiped awhile with the postmistress and, seizing the right opportunity, Stainless scrambled out."

"But how did he get back home again?"

"The next time Mrs. Driver went in for the groceries, of course. He was in a box of hair-combs at the time but he recognized the basket."

Arrietty looked thoughtful. "Poor Stainless," she said, after a moment, "what an experience! He must have been terrified."

"Terrified! Stainless! Not he! He'd enjoyed every minute of it!" Homily's voice rose. "He'd had one wild, wicked, wonderful, never-to-be-forgotten week of absolute, glorious freedom—living on jujubes, walnut-whips, chocolate bars, bulls-eyes, hundreds and thousands and still lemonade. And what had he done to deserve it?" The chiffon between Homily's fingers seemed to dance with indignation. "That's what we asked ourselves! We didn't like it. Not after all we'd been through: we never did think it was fair!" Crossly,

she shook out the chiffon and with lips set, began
to fold it. But gradually, as she smoothed her
hands across the frail silk, her movements became
more gentle: she looked thoughtful suddenly and,
as Arrietty watched, a little smile began to form
at the corners of her mouth. "There was one thing,
though, that we all noticed. . . ." she said after a
moment.

"What was that?" asked Arrietty.

"He'd lost his wonderful complexion."

THE ITALIAN BOY

Gillian Avery

BLANCHE AND WINIFRED INGRAM went to Italy in
the spring of 1878, when Blanche was eight years old
and Winifred thirteen, the only two children left
out of a family that had once been large. Blanche
was not even sure how many brothers and sisters
she might have had. Clothilde, Eugene and
Albertine, for instance, were just names on the
gravestone in the churchyard where her mother was
buried. She only knew that she had worn black
frocks all her life until the year they came to Italy,
when, very pleasantly, there did not seem to be
anybody else to die, and she and Winifred had
been given new dresses: grey merino and white
alpaca. Winifred had disapproved and had asked
that black braid should be sewn to both her dresses,

which had meant that Blanche had felt obliged to ask for the same, but even so, it had given her enormous pleasure to be dressed in white and grey. Winifred had wept and told her she was heartless to care so little about poor Mamma and Jessica, who had been the last sister to die. So after that Blanche had felt troubled and guilty, though there was nothing to be done; the old black dresses had been too small and had been taken away. All she could do, as Winifred was forever pointing out, was to look sad and serious when they walked together in the Boboli Gardens, and hold Wini-fred's hand tightly. Winifred herself wore a large black mourning brooch with strands of Mamma's hair in it. Blanche thought it very pretty, but she noticed that people did not nudge each other and stare now that they no longer were dressed in black. She had said something about this to Winifred, trying to explain that it was partly because of this that she was glad they had stopped wearing mourning. But Winifred had been very cross and Blanche had the feeling that she liked being looked at, though she only thought this for a moment because she knew Winifred could not be vain; vanity was a sin, Winifred was always telling her so.

Blanche did not like Italy. Winifred had told her when they first knew Papa was taking them to Florence that she would hate Italy, and that she would be homesick for London and English ways.

So Blanche had hated Italy from the first moment she had stepped off the train and had seen the dark-haired swarthy porters in their blue smocks ready to swoop down on the luggage and carry it off.

"Papa, Papa, they'll steal it!" she had cried, clinging to her father's arm.

"You see how frightened Blanche is already," remarked Winifred. "It won't be at all good for her being here. I'm sure the doctors were wrong, telling you to bring her to Italy."

But their father, abstractedly trying to pull his coat sleeve away from Blanche's tugging fingers, had said he was sure Blanche would enjoy Florence when she was used to it, and that the warmer climate would suit her health much better. Blanche did not need to think whether she liked it or not, because Winifred told her every day how horrible it was. The sun was too bright, there were no curtains but heavy shutters instead, the floors were stone, there were no proper trees, just dusty evergreens. Above all, the people were so dirty. Blanche had not noticed this for herself—the skins of the Italians seemed brown to her; but Winifred said that they were dirty and that no Italian washed.

Every day they walked from their apartment, along the river to the Boboli Gardens. They were too old for a nurse now, and besides everyone said how serious and responsible Winifred was. ("Look how she cares for Blanche—why, she hardly leaves the child for a moment.") Their French maid, Héloise, used to walk behind them, and in front would go Winifred, her head held high, her black mourning brooch pinned prominently on her dress, holding Blanche's hot sticky hand firmly.

The Boboli Gardens were very different from Kensington Gardens, where they walked when they were in London. They had to go past a huge palace to reach them, a palace that made Kensington Palace look quite small and cosy by comparison. There was a grotto, a sort of pretty cave where water dripped with a delicious tinkle; and a great number of interesting statues past which Winifred always hurried her. Then you reached the proper gardens. They stretched upwards in flights of terraces, a great contrast to the flat spaces of Kensington Gardens, and they were bordered with evergreen hedges which made shady lanes stretching up the hill. In nooks in the hedges were stone benches. In the middle of the garden was what Winifred told Blanche was an amphitheatre; a sweeping semi-circle of rising rows of stone seats which looked down on a patch of grass and gravel at the bottom. It would be fun, Blanche thought, to leap down those seats as though they were giant steps.

But she and Winifred never, of course, did anything of the sort. Winifred would find a stone bench in the shade of one of the evergreen trees, and there they would both sit with Héloise at the furthest end, engrossed in her knitting. Blanche's legs were too short to reach the ground and so she swung them and stared alternately at the dust on her black patent leather shoes and at the children playing nearby.

Many of the children who came to the Boboli Gardens were English children with their nurses and governesses. There was Herbert Danyell, for instance, with his little brothers and sisters, who lived on the Lungarno Soderini, very near where the Ingrams had their own apartment. He seemed a nice boy, Blanche thought, and she liked the way he was so kind to the little ones, and rolled a ball for them to play with. She would have liked to play with them herself; indeed, the Danyells' governess, who was a plump person with a kind face, had once come up to the sisters to suggest that Blanche might care to join in. But Winifred had spoken for her.

"Thank you, my sister does not care to play, do you, Blanche?" Blanche, gazing up with sad eyes, had nodded, and the governess had gone away.

After that, Blanche could hardly bear to look at the Danyells playing so merrily with their hoops and balls. She used to stare instead at the brown-skinned Italian children who squatted down and picked buttercups in the grass near the stone pool, or who leapt about chasing the butterflies that drifted through the warm air.

Then one day Herbert Danyell himself came

running up to their bench. "Can you come to my birthday party on Thursday week?" he had said breathlessly. "Mamma says that it is to be fancy dress this time, and I'm going to go as a soldier. The dressmaker's making my costume now, and there's a real sword with a sharp blade."

It was a proper invitation, because the governess had come up behind Herbert and repeated it. Only she of course had given the date and the time and had said that Mrs. Danyell had written a proper card. Blanche had looked desperately at Winifred, clutching her hands so that her nails dug into the flesh of her palm. Her breath had come out in a little gust of disappointment when Winifred had said, "But I am afraid that is impossible. You see, my sister and I are still in mourning."

This time the governess had not been daunted. She looked at their white alpaca dresses and said she was sorry, she had understood from Mrs. Danyell that the mourning was over now. Perhaps Mrs. Danyell would speak to the Ingrams' papa. Blanche knew that it was no good her speaking to Winifred about the matter, but she had prayed hard all the way home, her lips moving, her eyes fixed straight, unseeing, ahead, so that she had tripped and stumbled, and had once walked into a lamp-post.

Her prayers were heard. A beautiful invitation card came with gilded edges, and with it a note addressed to Mr. Ingram. Mr. Ingram rarely tried to tell Winifred what to do, but this time he was firm.

"I should like you to go. It would be difficult to refuse without hurting Mrs. Danyell's feelings, and there is really no reason why you should not begin to go about a little more. It is quite a year since. . . ." Here Mr. Ingram hesitated, then he went on, "and I am sure Mamma would have wished it."

"But Papa," cried Winifred, "you aren't making allowances for *our* feelings! *We* never forget Mamma, whatever other people do." Sobbing, she rushed out of the room. She stayed in the bedroom for hours; Blanche could hear her blowing her nose, so she knew she was crying. Blanche herself hovered miserably outside the door. All her pleasure in the party had vanished. Instead she felt guiltily that if she had not prayed so hard none of this would have happened.

But the next morning Winifred seemed calm and composed. "Since you wish us to go to Mrs. Danyell's party, then we must, Papa. But I think we should still wear mourning. Blanche and I will dress in black velvet as the little princes who died in the Tower of London. There is a picture in Blanche's history book that the dressmaker can copy."

The odd thing was that Winifred took increasing pleasure in the thought of the party. She delighted in the visits to the dressmaker, where she inspected and rejected materials, criticized, gave instructions, tried on half-finished parts of the costume, and examined herself in the huge looking glass. But Blanche's pleasure dwindled. She hated all the fitting that was needed, she hated having to stand still for so long while Signora Luchesi groped round her with a mouthful of pins, and above all, she hated wearing black. When Herbert had talked about fancy dress she had immediately thought of herself in gay colours, an eighteenth-century lady in pink and green satin perhaps, or a columbine, or a character from a fairy story. And now here she was, back in that horrible black, dressed as something from her hated history book. Moreover Winifred was making her rehearse the part every day, and it had not taken Blanche long to discover that all she was going to be allowed to do at the party was to hold Winifred's hand, to cling to her arm and rest her head on her shoulder and look sad and frightened.

"But it will be just like the old days," wailed Blanche, "when we were in mourning."

"But think how nice you'll be," said Winifred, "with your hair all combed out and a gold chain. And two of us, all in black, we'll look so interesting. Everybody will turn to look."

"I don't *want* them to look at me, that's what they always used to do. Besides, I thought it was vain to want people to take notice of you."

This made Winifred very angry. She went

scarlet, said Blanche didn't know what she was talking about, and even shook her a little. Blanche felt guiltily that she had gone too far. She decided that she must try not to grumble any more, even when the pins that the Signora stuck into the hem pricked her legs.

The costumes were difficult to make, and the Signora would have to work at them until the last moment. In fact she could not deliver them until the evening before the party. But when the day came the arrival of the costumes was driven to the back of their minds by something very disturbing. Blanche was to go for her afternoon walk without Winifred.

Since Mamma's last illness the two sisters had hardly been separated for five minutes. They slept together, Winifred helped Blanche with her lessons and Blanche sat by while Winifred had hers with visiting masters. "She is my responsibility," Winifred would say. "There is nobody else to bring her up."

But now some invalid English lady living up at Fiesole, an old friend of their mother's, had asked to see Winifred. She had not asked for Blanche; she probably did not even know of Blanche's existence, so Mr. Ingram said she must stay behind. On the other hand, he insisted that Winifred should go up to Fiesole. It was the least she could do for somebody who had been so fond of dear Mamma. Winifred was very upset at leaving

Blanche, though after Mamma's name had been mentioned in this way she had not been able to protest any more. However, she said she thought it would be as well if Blanche stayed at home while she was out.

"You see, she never goes out without me, Papa. She might be frightened. You don't want to go out without Winifred, do you, Blanche?"

But here again Mr. Ingram was unexpectedly firm. "Then I think she should learn to go without you. She isn't a baby any more, and Héloise is perfectly capable of looking after her."

So Blanche had seen the carriage roll away with Winifred and Papa sitting side by side, Winifred with her golden hair flowing down her back and a black hat with a little black feather. Then she and Héloise walked along the road by the river to the Boboli Gardens. Blanche felt so odd and strange without Winifred that she wondered everybody did not turn round and stare—as though she had come out without clothes. There was nobody to hold her tightly by the hand; she could swing her arms as much as she liked. If she loitered, then Héloise loitered too; nobody told her to hurry up. She even ventured to lean on the parapet by the side of the river and look down at the wistaria that climbed up the walls and sniff up the delicious scent. Héloise did not remonstrate, she just stood and waited.

It was the same when they reached the Gardens.

Héloise allowed her to linger near all the statues, including a very rude one of a fat man with a tortoise, which Blanche knew Winifred would have thought wicked, and which gave her, because of that, a delightful sense of naughtiness when she gazed at it. ("But," she argued with herself, "Héloise is in charge of me. She is grown up and knows what things are wrong. So if she doesn't stop me then it's all right.")

They climbed up to their usual bench, and there Héloise sat down and took out her knitting, and Blanche sat and drew patterns in the gravel with the toes of her shoes. The Danyells were not there this afternoon, but the Winningtons were, a family of girls whom they knew slightly. They were playing with a shuttlecock, which flew about so lightly and so easily that Blanche longed for a racket to try to hit it too. Then Héloise looked up.

"Why do you not join your friends?" she remarked.

Blanche stared at her. The daring of the suggestion made her speechless. Héloise must know that she and Winifred never played. But if a grown-up gave permission it was not for a child to argue. Slowly she got to her feet, still staring at Héloise, wondering if she really meant it.

Héloise nodded. "Run down to your friends. Away."

Blanche did not run, she went slowly down the huge steps of the amphitheatre. She did not know the Winningtons at all well, and she was wondering how she was going to ask to play with them. Nobody noticed her when she arrived down on the gravel. All four children were playing, hitting the feathered shuttlecock from one to another, round in a ring, concentrating hard, watching it anxiously as it bounded up and down. Nor did their nurse-maid notice Blanche; she was busily talking to a nurse from one of the other English families. Blanche felt lonely, and glanced back at Héloise. But she had spread a book on her knees now and did not look up.

Then suddenly somebody spoke at Blanche's elbow, and she swung round. It was an Italian boy, of about her own age. He was watching the flight of the shuttlecock, and every time it leapt off one of the children's rackets and flew up into the air he laughed as though he had never seen anything so delightful and so funny. Blanche could not help laughing too, partly because of the boy beside her, but also because of the joy of seeing the shuttle-cock soar up yet another time when you felt sure that its flight must be coming to an end. Then at last the youngest Winnington let it fall. Blanche turned to the boy.

"Isn't it sad?" She suddenly felt as though she had known him all her life. "Poor shuttlecock. I wish it could have gone on flying for ever, like a bird."

Then she remembered that she was talking to a

stranger, an Italian boy, and she gave a little gasp and put her fingers on her mouth. He must be Italian, he could not possibly be one of the English children. He had a pale brown skin and the most beautiful black, crisp hair that waved all over his head, and very white teeth. His shirt was patched, and so were his trousers, and though he was not barefooted, like some of the Italian children, he must have been wearing his father's shoes, for they were very large indeed. But he did not look in the least dirty (Winifred said all Italians were dirty), and he had a most friendly smile. He smiled now and pointed to the yellow butterflies that fluttered lazily over the grass where the buttercups grew.

"Let's chase them," said Blanche gleefully, and she ran boldly on to the grass.

But they were far more difficult to catch than she would ever have thought. She would creep up on one as it rested with folded wings on a buttercup, and then just as her two hands were put out to cup it, it would flutter slowly away, only an inch or two beyond her fingertips. But her companion caught one. As she was standing frustrated and weary he came up with clasped hands, and moved his thumbs so that she could see, between his palms, an imprisoned butterfly.

"Oh let it go, you'll hurt it so," Blanche cried in an agony, tugging at his arm. He smiled, pulled his hands apart, and the butterfly soared out. They watched until it was lost in the air.

"I know," said Blanche, "let's play hide and seek. Among those hedges." She pointed to the lanes of dark evergreens that went up the hill. But he smiled back at her uncomprehendingly, and she realized he did not understand. "Like this," she said coaxingly, and ran and crouched down behind a bush and called "Coo-ee." Then he understood and came after her, and she ran away laughing.

Up and down those sloping pathways they ran through the hot afternoon. Blanche thought that never in her life had she been so happy. She had not known that any companion could play so beautifully as this, and the paths seemed to have been made specially for hide and seek. It was the perfection of happiness to crouch down behind a stone bench, the warm pungent smell of the evergreens in her nose, waiting with a loudly beating heart for the boy's footsteps. Sometimes they would pass slowly on the other side of the hedge, and there was a thrilling excitement in knowing that for the moment he had not seen her. Sometimes they would hesitate and then quicken and come nearer, and her heart felt as though it would burst out of her body, and she would crouch lower and lower and try to curl herself into a tight ball like a hedgehog in her efforts not to be seen.

She remembered Héloise, though. From time to time she would go up to the bench, trying to smooth down her hair and wipe her wet forehead. "Is it all right to go on playing?" she would ask.

"Is it time to go home yet?" But even though the bench was in the shadow now, Héloise, hardly raising her eyes from her book, would say that there was still time for a little more play. So Blanche would go off sedately at first, then break into a run to join her companion. She was doing her best, she told herself, she was giving Héloise a chance to forbid her playing.

At last, however, Héloise, shutting her book with a sigh, said that they must go. There were long shadows over the gardens now, and the English families had all gone home to their teas. While Héloise put away her knitting Blanche crept off to the hedge where the Italian boy was standing. "I have got to go home now," she said sadly. "But come home with me and then you'll see where we live." To make him understand, she pointed into the distance, and then made beckoning movements.

He seemed to know what she meant, for when she set off with Héloise she saw him standing and watching and then following. All the way home she kept peeping over her shoulder. There he was still, a few paces behind; she would giggle, and he would wave and laugh. Blanche's happiness remained with her. The smell of wistaria drifted up from the river bank, the Arno shone in the late afternoon sun, and on the far side the towers and domes of Florence stood out against the pale blue sky. Bells sounded across the water, and Blanche suddenly realized with astonishment that in spite of Winifred, she liked Florence.

When they reached the gates of the stone court, where you went in to reach the apartment, Blanche dawdled behind and waved good-bye. Then rushing past Héloise she ran as fast as she could up the stairs to the apartment, and into the bedroom she shared with Winifred. She heard the voice of Mrs. Martin, their English cook, calling to her. "There's a nice surprise for two little ladies. Just you look inside the boxes the Signora sent round this afternoon. There's one on each bed."

It was the costumes, the prince in the Tower costumes, of course, but Blanche did not bother to look at them. She flew over to the window, wrestled with the heavy shutters, and then managed to throw one back with a bang against the wall. There he was, leaning against the parapet of the river, looking up in her direction and shading his eyes against the evening sun. "Coo-ee," shouted Blanche, and waved. Even at that distance she could see him smiling as he waved back.

At that moment Blanche loved him so much that it almost hurt. What could she give him to show him how much she had enjoyed that afternoon in the Gardens? She turned and looked feverishly round the room. There was so little in it that was theirs—clothes, brushes, their prayer books, nothing more. Then her eyes fell on the boxes. She tore open the one that had been left on her bed. There was a mass of rustling white paper and she pulled out the black silk shirt, the velvet tunic trimmed with fur, the black silk stockings, the gold-embroidered black shoes, the gold chain. Pulling off the paper and scattering it on the floor, she gathered the clothes in her arms. Down the stone staircase she ran. The stockings trailed on the ground and she was afraid she might trip over them but she dared not stop in case she was too late for the boy. But when she peeped out of the gates into the road he was still there. "Come here," she called, "I've got something for you." He crossed to the gates and she thrust the bundle into his arms. "It's for you. To wear. I want you to have it."

She watched his face. He fingered the clothes slowly, and looked at her, puzzled. "It's for you," she insisted, and pointed at him. He went on fingering them, and rubbed first the silk and then the velvet against his cheek. His face looked bright with pleasure now. Then he said something quickly to her, and ran behind a huge bush that was growing in a tub in the court. Blanche thought that perhaps he was playing hide and seek, and waited anxiously for him to say "coo-ee". She waited and waited, and hid her eyes so that she might not see where he had gone. Footsteps tiptoed near her, she laughed a little, but kept her eyes hidden. Then a hand touched her arm, and she looked up.

There stood the boy, but how grand he looked! Like a real king, like one of the portraits Mr.

Ingram had taken them to see in the Uffizi gallery. She had never realized when the Signora groped round her with pins and tacking threads that she was making something so splendid. Or perhaps it was because the boy himself had a face like a king. His back was so straight, he carried his head so high, he had his hand on his hip. Blanche knew that she could never have looked like that.

"You look like the grandest king there ever was," she said breathlessly, walking all round him. She was so absorbed that she never noticed the sound of carriage wheels approaching, stopping outside the court. Then all at once she heard Winifred's outraged voice.

"Why, Blanche! Papa, here's Blanche all by herself with a strange boy. Blanche, what are you doing? Where's Héloise?"

Then Blanche came to herself, out of the afternoon's long dream. "Go on," she said urgently to the boy. "You'll have to go." She made shooing gestures at him.

But he did not hurry. He picked up a bundle, the clothes he had taken off, made a superb bow to Blanche, and walked slowly off, past Winifred, past Mr. Ingram who was coming into the court at that moment. Winifred stared aghast, and then shook Blanche's arm. "Blanche, who is he? Why's he wearing those clothes? Answer me at once!"

"It's my costume," said Blanche defiantly. "My prince in the Tower costume. I've given it to him.

I wanted him to have it. He's the person I like best in the whole world."

It was only then that Winifred realized just what had happened. "Papa, Papa," she screamed. "Stop that boy, he's gone off with our costume. I think Blanche must have gone mad, she's wicked, I never knew anybody could be so wicked and so naughty. Papa, go and get him!" She tugged at his arm in a frenzy.

Blanche stared at them. She did not feel in the least sorry, though she felt surprised at her own behaviour. "You can't ask for it back," she remarked coolly. "I gave it to him, and Winifred always says people must never ask for things back." She dodged past her father and sister and went out into the street.

There was the boy, some distance away now, but strolling along as serenely as if he had been a real king. And it was she who had helped make him look so splendid! As she watched he turned and waved his hand. Excitedly she waved back and then turned to Winifred.

"He was an Italian boy, and he wasn't dirty. I love him, and I love Italy and I want to stay here all my life. Everything you told me was wrong, and it always has been wrong!"

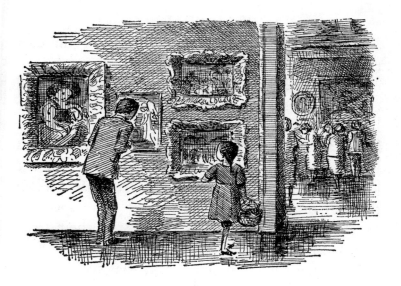

THE GOLD ANGEL

Eilís Dillon

ONE O'CLOCK was the best time of the day. At that hour, winter and summer, Luisa took her father his lunch at the picture gallery where he worked. He could have brought it with him in the morning but Luisa's mother liked to make sure that the bread and sausage were quite fresh and the wine cool. Also, her father liked to have a reason for seeing Luisa.

His name was Marco and he was an attendant at the picture gallery. At eight o'clock every morning he and the other attendants brushed and dusted the long rooms and saw that all the notices were in position. There were a great many notices, with directions about where to go next and how to find the way out. It was a very complicated building, and no one but the attendants and the director really knew their way all around it.

At nine o'clock the great doors were opened and the people who were already standing outside were let in. Most of them had guide-books in their hands and they went slowly through all the rooms looking up at the high pictures and down at the low pictures until their heads were dizzy. Then they sat down on the benches put there specially by the director for them, and rested their tired feet. Coming out they always said:

"What a day! It's hard work, that's what it is, going around a picture gallery."

When school was on, Luisa just had time to run home and take the basket which her mother had ready for her, and bring it to the gallery. There one by one the attendants went off to their little room and ate quickly. The gallery remained open all during the time when most people are eating at home, so as to give everyone a good chance of seeing the pictures. At four o'clock it closed for the rest of the day.

Luisa watched her father eating so that she would be able to tell her mother that he had finished everything. At the end he always said:

"Nothing like bread and sausage and wine. Tell your mother it was a fine lunch."

Then she would take the basket home.

When the holidays began she did not have to hurry. Often she came earlier than one o'clock so

as to have a look at the pictures. There was one
that she loved specially. It hung in the second long
room that she had to pass through, on her way to
the attendants' room. It was quite a small picture,
of a towering angel with a gold robe and wide
white wings. He was looking downwards. His
arms were stretched out towards a girl who sat in a
high-backed chair with an open book on her lap.
The angel was looking at the girl's face, and you
looked first at the angel and then at the girl. She
had the loveliest face that Luisa had ever seen, except for her sister Maria who was eighteen years old.

Maria worked in a shop that sold necklaces and
brooches and ear-rings. The owner of the shop said
that she brought him lots of business. People
looked in the window at the shining glass beads.
Then they saw Maria and came in for a closer look,
and they usually ended by buying something for
their own girls. All day long Maria put on one
necklace after the other, turning this way and that
to show how well it would suit Anna or Laura or
Francesca, or another Maria.

One day, at lunch-time, when Luisa went
through the long room with her basket, she saw
that a young man was standing in front of her picture. He was so intent on it that she tiptoed past
so as not to disturb his enjoyment of it. He did not
move. His eyes were fixed on the seated girl in the
picture, so fiercely that Luisa almost expected her
to lift her gaze from her book and look back at him.

Luisa did not mention the young man to her father. Everywhere in the gallery, there were people looking in admiration at the pictures. She had only noticed the young man because he was admiring her special one.

The next day he was there again, at the same time. Now she noticed that he carried a leather case, as if he were on his way home from work. This meant that he lived near the gallery, perhaps as near as she did herself. She walked slowly past him, but very quietly, so as to see his face. He was thin, and rather tall, though his shoulders were hunched forward so as to bring him closer to the picture. All she saw of his face was two burning dark-brown eyes, when he moved a little.

For several more days she saw him, always in the same place. No one else seemed to have noticed that he gave all his attention to one picture when he came to the gallery. She asked her father if it happened often that people came in just to see one picture.

"Sometimes," he said. "Or it can happen that they come in to look at everything and then one picture seems to stop them and they have to stay and look only at that one. I've seen that happen with the portrait of Lorenzo the Magnificent. I've seen people trying to get away from him and still he keeps pulling them back with his eyes. The director is going to put a bench in front of him, to save those poor people's feet."

"Is it always portraits that do that?"

"Sometimes it's portraits and sometimes it's the background of a picture—a road winding up and up through olive trees and cypresses, perhaps. People seem to wander along the road and not be able to get off it, until you would think I'd have to go in there after them and haul them out, at closing time."

"Does it make them happy to look at the pictures like that?"

"What does it matter whether they're happy or not? It's good for them."

But the young man looked very unhappy and Luisa could not believe that it was good for him. Since she had seen him first, he seemed to have grown even thinner. Perhaps he had begun to fear that his interest in that one picture would be noticed, because now he always looked at one or two others near it as well. But always he came back to the first one again.

One day, as Luisa was passing him by, she saw that he was standing at one side of the picture, peering along the wall at it. There was no one near him in the long room. The attendant had gone into the next room, because at lunchtime each man's charge was doubled so as to give everyone a chance to eat in turn. Without lifting her eyes, Luisa knew that the man was looking to see how the picture was hung.

She felt a little dart of anger go through her. So

this was all his interest: he did not love the picture
at all but was only planning to steal it. For a
moment she hated him for this so much that she
wanted to run to her father and tell him what she
feared. Then she recovered herself and thought:

"He wants to see that picture from every point.
He wants to know everything about it. Why
should he fix on that picture to steal? There are
plenty of others, worth a lot more."

But she knew that he might have fixed on that
one because it was small and easily carried. It was
painted on wood, and it would be light, because it
had no frame. He would know this if he had stolen
pictures before. She had seen how he had looked at
the picture with love, but perhaps it was love of the
money that he would get for it that had shown so
clearly.

Still she could not bring herself to tell her father
that a man in the long room was planning to steal
the blue and gold angel. It seemed to her that the
angel himself would not have allowed that.

But the next day he did steal it.

Luisa could hardly believe her eyes. She was
coming back from the attendants' room with her
empty basket. Her father had called the other
attendant to tell him that he had finished his lunch.
In that moment when there was no one to watch
him, the man just lifted the picture off the wall
and began quietly to carry it towards the door. It
did not seem to trouble him that several people

were standing about looking at other pictures. He was quite right in this. No one took any notice of him except Luisa.

She had no time to think. Like a flash she ran out of the room by the upper door and along the corridor that went by the side of the angel's room. At the end of it was the gold-painted notice on a stand, saying: "This way out." She left that one, but when she came to the next one she moved it a little, and the next, and the next. Then she stood in a doorway in this dim and quiet part of the building and waited.

It was agony to wait. He was not a stupid thief. Perhaps he would remember the way out. Perhaps he was already on the street, on his way to sell the angel.

But in a moment she heard his soft steps sounding in the passageway. Only a yard away, he walked quietly past her. Then he started down the stairs at the end. She followed him now. She could see the top of his head go lower and lower. Then it stopped. He had noticed that something was wrong. She was at the head of the stairs now. She stood quite still and waited.

Slowly he turned around. Behind him was the locked door of the room where the attendants kept their brushes. There was no way out except by the stairs where Luisa stood. She wondered if he would come plunging up the stairs and knock her down, and make off with the picture after all. Very softly she said: "Keep quiet and I won't tell on you."

"Who are you?"

"I'm the daughter of one of the attendants. I've been watching you for days."

"I saw you, but you're only a child."

Luisa said:

"I won't always be one. And I can run fast. If you move, I'll be quicker than you. I'll call everyone and they'll catch you at the door."

"So what am I to do?" the man said bitterly. "If we stay here long enough, someone will surely come."

"We won't stay long. I want to know, was it your own idea to steal the picture or did someone send you?"

"It was my own idea."

"Had you arranged for someone to buy it from you?"

"No." He paused and then said suddenly: "I wasn't going to sell it at all. I was going to keep it."

"Why?"

"To look at. To have. I can only come at lunchtime. The gallery shuts at four o'clock. If I could have it the whole evening—now I can only see it for an hour at my lunchtime."

"When do you eat?"

"In the evening."

"Where do you live, then? With your wife, or your mother?"

"I'm alone, in a room—what are you asking questions for? You're too curious."

"Anyone would be curious about you, you do such queer things. No lunch, only look at a picture!"

"It's better than lunch to me."

"Perhaps, but you won't get fat on it."

"I don't care about that. I only want the picture."

"Why?"

The young man stared at her for a moment as if he were blind. Then he said:

"You may as well know it. You know enough about me, if you have been watching me for days. I've got to tell someone, or I'll start telling people in the street, or even go in—go in and tell the girl herself."

He went into a shocked silence at this thought. Luisa said softly:

"What girl?"

"There is a shop two streets away from here, where they sell necklaces and ear-rings and bracelets. There is a girl there, the loveliest girl in the whole world. Every day I watched her through the glass, arranging the things, talking to the customers, and I know she is not only lovely on the outside. She is good and gentle and serious."

"Why did you never talk to her?"

"Perhaps I would have, but one day the owner of the shop came out while I was watching and asked me if I wanted to buy something. When I said that I did not, he said that anyway Maria was not for sale. And he laughed. I wanted to land him sitting in the gutter for laughing but I just went away. Since then, I come here instead and look at the picture. It's so like her—"

"Yes, but it's a dead thing!" Luisa would never have believed that she could talk so of her picture. "I know Maria. It will be better to talk to her than to steal a picture—"

"I wasn't stealing it," he began indignantly. Suddenly his eyes fell to the picture which he still clutched, and he looked like a man who has picked up a snake by mistake. "I *stole* it! Of course I did! What can I do now?"

"Give it to me," said Luisa. "Everyone that matters is at lunch. If I'm seen carrying it, it will be thought that I have been sent with it. Now go out quietly—I'll show you the way—quickly—and come back to-morrow at the same time—to the long room—hurry!"

By this time, other visitors to the gallery had followed the changed notices and footsteps could be heard approaching the stairs. Luisa took the picture under her arm and started back along the passageway.

"This is not the way out," she explained politely to wondering groups of visitors. "I'll show you."

And she led them back to the main hallway, casually turning the notices to their correct posi-

tions as she went. Then she walked quietly back
to the long room and hung the gold angel on his
hook again. The attendant came in as she
finished straightening it, calling excitedly over his
shoulder:

"It's gone—you'll see, it's gone!"

Then he stopped, and his mouth and eyes opened
wider and wider so that Luisa burst out laughing.

"It was gone," the attendant said in a weak
voice.

"Well, it's there now," said Marco, Luisa's
father. "We all know there are ghosts in this
gallery."

The other attendant looked angry but there was
nothing more to be said.

In the evening, before closing time, Luisa went
to the shop to talk with Maria. She was wearing a
long pearl necklace with a shining clasp. The pearls
glowed with a white light, and they seemed to flow
around her long neck. A little fat man was buying
them for his wife's fiftieth birthday, and he watched
carefully while Maria turned this way and that to
show them off.

"They will be beautiful," the little man said,
"though my wife is a bigger woman."

Maria put the necklace in a box and wrapped it
up while Luisa waited. When the little man had
gone, she said:

"They always say the same thing. All the little
fat men buy pearl necklaces when their wives are

fifty years old. They can't afford them when they are younger."

Luisa said:

"Did you ever notice a thin young man who looked through the window at you?"

Maria blushed and said:

"Yes, but he doesn't come any more. And he never spoke."

"He is ready to speak now," said Luisa. "You had better come to the gallery tomorrow at lunch time. He'll be there, in the long room, by the gold angel."

"But I don't know him," Maria said. "He only looked through the window."

"That doesn't matter. I know him very well indeed. Do you want him to die?"

And because she did not want him to die, Maria came to the gallery.

GABBLE-GABBLE

James Reeves

"Gabble-gabble! gabble-gabble!"
The seven fat geese say.
"Gabble-gabble! gabble-gabble!"
In the green field all day.

"Gabble-gabble"—never stopping,
While the sun sweeps the sky.
Gabble-gabble go the seven geese,
And I will tell you why.

Those seven geese sat in the hot sun
In the meadow long ago,
And through the hedge came the red fox
And spied them all in a row.

"Ho ho!" said he with a wicked grin
And a glint in his hungry eye.
"I never saw such a dinner before,
And today those geese must die!"

"Oh no, Sir Fox, have pity on us!"
They cried with anguish shrill.
"Sir Fox," they begged, "it is not right
Such poor weak birds to kill."

"Fat, foolish geese, your wailing cease,"
Said the red fox in his greed.
"Fat, foolish geese, prepare to die;
Your plaints I will not heed."

"Oh then, Sir Fox," the first goose said,
"If our lives you will not spare,
Take us and eat us one and all,
But first let us say a prayer.

"Gladly we give ourselves to you
When we have prayed to Heaven
For we shall be the sweeter fare
If our sins be forgiven."

"A pious thought," the fox agreed.
"Pray on, pray on, I say!
I will not touch you, foolish geese,
Till you have ceased to pray."

So "gabble-gabble" the seven geese prayed
From sunrise to sunset.
"Gabble-gabble" to Heaven they cried
And have not left off yet.

THE CHIEF'S DAUGHTER

Rosemary Sutcliff

THE DUN, the Strong-Place, stood far out on the headland, seeming almost to overhang the Western Sea. Three deep turf banks ringed it round, and where the hawthorn stakes of the stockade had taken root here and there, their small stunted branches with salt-burned leaves grew bent all one way by the sea wind.

The Chief's big round Hall where the Fire of the Clan never died on the hearth, stood at the highest part of the enclosure, with his byres and barns and stables, and the women's huts clumped about it. But in quiet times only the Chief himself and his kindred and household warriors lived there, while the rest of the Clan lived in the stone and turf bothies scattered over the landward side of the headland. Only when the raiders came out of the West in their skin-covered war boats, would the whole Clan drive their cattle into the spaces between the sheltering turf banks, and take refuge in the Chief's stronghold.

It was such a time now, the whole enclosure crowded with men and women and children and dogs and lean pigs, while the cattle lowed and fidgeted uneasily in their cramped space. For three days ago, the war boats had come again, and the Irish raiders were loose along the coast of Wales, scouring the hills for cattle and slaves.

On the sloping roof of the hut where the black herd bull lived, a boy and a girl were sprawling side by side. The boy would rather have climbed to the roof of the Hall, because from there you could get a further view to the west, but the turf of the Hall roof, tawny as a hound's coat, was growing slippery with the dryness of late summer, while the bull-house was thatched with heather that gave you something to dig your toes and heels into, so that you did not keep sliding off all the time.

The girl was ten years old, dark and slight, like most of the folk in the headland Strong-Place below her. She had found a grey and white seagull's feather caught in the rough thatch, and was trying to twist it into her long dark hair. The boy, who lay propped on one elbow staring out to sea, was older, with hair and eyes almost the same colour as the string of amber round his neck. He did not belong to the girl's People, but was a prisoner in their hands, left behind wounded, the last time the Irish war boats came.

The girl gave up trying to make the feather stay in her hair, and sat chewing the end of it instead. "Dara, why will you always be staring out toward the sunset?"

The boy went on staring. "I look towards my home."

"If you loved it so much, why did you leave it and come raiding in ours?"

He shrugged. "I am a man. When the other men go raiding, should I sit at home spinning with the women?"

"A *man*! You're only twelve, even now! Only two years older than I am!"

That time the boy did not answer at all. The sea creamed on the rocks under the headland, and from beneath the heather thatch came the soft heavy puffing of the herd bull. After a while the girl threw the feather away, and said crossly, "All right, go on staring into the sunset. *I* am not wanting to talk to you."

"Why should you want to talk to a prisoner?" Dara snapped, looking round at last. "You did not have to come climbing up here after me."

"You would not have been even a prisoner, if I had not pleaded for you. They meant to sacrifice you to the Black Mother; you know that, don't you?"

"I know that. You've reminded me often enough," Dara said between his teeth. "It is a great honour that Nessan the Chief's daughter should plead for me. I must remember and be grateful."

The girl seemed to have got over her sudden crossness, and looked at him consideringly. "Yes, I think you should," she said after a moment, "for besides pleading for you with Father *and* with Laethrig the Priest, I gave my best blue glass arm-ring to the Mother, that she might not be angry with us for keeping you alive!"

And then someone came past the bull-house with a clanking pail, and looked up and called to Dara that it was time he came down and took his share of the work, for the cattle needed watering.

Just below the Chief's Hall, where the land began to drop, a spring burst out from under a grey boulder. It filled a small deep pool almost like a well, then spilled over and away down the narrow gulley it had worn for itself, through the gap left for it in the encircling banks, and dropped over the cliff edge making a thread of white water among the rocks, until it reached the sea. That evening it seemed to the men watering the cattle that it was running unusually low, and when the pails were brought up out of the well-pool, it took longer than usual to refill. Some of them looked at each other a little anxiously. But the spring had never been known to dry up, no matter how many men and cattle drank from it. They were imagining things . . . It would be its usual self in the morning. . . .

But in the morning, when it was time to water the cattle again, and the women came to draw the day's pitcher-full for their households, there was scarcely any water spilling over into the little gully at all.

"It has been a dry summer, I am thinking," one woman said.

Another shook her head. "We have had dry summers before."

"It is in my mind," said a man standing by with a pail for his cattle, "that this thing must be told quickly to the Chief."

The Chief came, and looked into the sullen stillness of the well, and then up into the heat-milky sky, pulling the dark front-locks of hair on either side of his face as he always did when troubled. "It must surely rain soon," he said after a while. "Maybe rain is all we need. But meanwhile the cattle must be doing with half measure, and see that the women take their pitchers away only half full."

What he did not say, and no one else said either, for even to speak of such a thing would be unlucky, was, "If the water fails, the stronghold fails also."

All that day the people went about with anxious eyes, returning again and again to look at the spring.

By evening, the pool had barely filled up again, and not one drop was spilling over into the stony runnel.

Then the Chieftain sent for Laethrig the Priest. And Laethrig came, very old and brittle, like a withered leaf, in his mantle of beaver skins with his necklaces of dried seed pods and slender sea-bird bones rustling and rattling about his neck. And he sat down beside the spring and went away small inside himself so that looking into his eyes was like looking through the doorway of an empty hut. And it seemed a long time, to the men and women waiting about him, before he came back and looked out of his eyes again.

"What is it?" they asked, softly like a little wind through the headland grasses. "What is it, Old Wise One?"

The old man said, "It is as I feared. The Black Mother is angry with us because we did not slay in her honour the Irish captive."

The Chieftain had grown fond of the red-haired boy, and a shadow crossed his face, but he only said, "The Will of the Goddess is the Will of the Goddess. What must we do, Old Wise One?"

Laethrig the Priest got slowly to his feet, and drew his beaver-skin mantle about him. "At first dark, we must begin to cry to the Goddess, on the sacred drums, and at moon-set we must make the sacrifice. Then the Black Mother will no longer be angry with us, and she will give us back the living water, so that our spring will run full again."

Nessan, on the outskirts of the crowd, had the sudden dreadful feeling of being tangled in a bad dream. In the dream she saw Dara standing quite still in the grip of the huge warrior who had caught hold of him. He looked more bewildered than afraid, and she thought that he had not really understood what Laethrig said. He and she could manage well enough when they talked together, but the tongue of the Irish raiders was different in many ways from the tongue that her own people spoke, and he might not have understood.

Despite the hot evening, her feet seemed to have frozen to the ground, and she could not move or make a sound; and still in the bad dream she saw them take Dara away. She knew that he had begun to be afraid now; he looked back once as though with a desperate hope that someone would help him. And then he was gone.

Nessan unfroze, and her head began to work again. It whirled with thoughts and half-ideas chasing each other round and round, while she still hovered on the edge of the murmuring crowd. And then quite suddenly, out of the chase and whirl, a plan began to come, detail after detail, until she knew exactly what she must do.

The three Drummers of the Clan stepped into the open space beside the spring, and began to make a soft eery whispering and throbbing with their finger tips on the sacred wolfskin drums, and all the Clan who were not already there, came gathering as though at a call. The sun was down and the shadows crowding in, made sharp-edged and thin by the moon, as she slipped away unnoticed by the crowd. The rest of the Dun was almost deserted now; no one to notice her as she slipped by like another shadow. She ran to the place where the stream gully zigzagged out through its gap at the cliff's edge—everything depended on that— then to the out-shed where tomorrow's bread was stored; then to a certain dark bothie among the sleeping-places. It was easy to find the right one, for the huge warrior who had taken Dara away stood on guard before its door-hole, leaning on his spear. Her heart was beating right up in her throat as she started to work her way round to the back of the bothie, so that she was sure only the throbbing of the drums kept the spear man from hearing it, and was terrified that they might stop.

But she reached the back of the bothie, and checked there, carefully thinking out her next move.

Many of the living huts had a loose strip of turf in the roof, which could be turned back to let in more air in hot summer weather, and by good fortune, this was one of them. She reached up (the rough stone walls were so low that the edge of the roof came down to only just above her head) and felt for the rope of twisted heather that held the loose end of the summer-strip in place, and found it. She pulled it free, but standing on the ground, she could not reach up far enough to raise the turf flap more than a few fingers' lengths. Well, that did not matter, so long as she could get a hand inside. She got a good hold on the top of the hut wall; it was easy enough to find a toe-hold in a chink between two stones, and she was as light as a cat. Next instant she was crouching belly-flat along the edge of the roof, listening for any sound from the man on the far side of the hut.

No sound came. She found the edge of the summer-strip again, and lifted it a little and then a little more, until she could let it fold back on itself, with no more sound than a mouse might have made in the thatch.

In the pitch darkness below the square hole, she thought she heard quick breathing and then a tiny startled movement. She ducked her head and shoulders inside. "Dara! It's me—Nessan."

And Dara's voice whispered back, "Nessan!"

"Don't make a sound! There's a man with a spear outside. Have they tied you up?"

"Yes—to the house-post."

"I am coming down." Nessan felt for the right hold, and swung her legs into the hole, and dropped. Any sound that she made was covered by the wolfskin drums which woke at that moment into a coughing roar. Then she had found Dara and pulled her little food knife from her belt and was feeling for the rawhide ropes that lashed his hands behind him to the tall centre pole of the bothie.

"What does it all mean?" he whispered. "What have I done?"

"They say the Black Mother is angry, and that is why the spring is failing. They say that they must kill you at moon-set tonight, and then she will not be angry any more."

Dara gave a gasp, and jerked in his bonds.

"Hold still, or I shall cut you! But they shan't do it! I will not let them!"

"How can you stop them?" Dara's voice shook a little in the dark. "Go away, Nessan—go away before they find you!"

Nessan didn't bother to answer that. She went on sawing at the rawhide ropes, until suddenly the last strand parted. She gave a little sound like a whimper, under her breath. "There. Now come!"

She could feel him rubbing his wrists to get the feeling back. "You first; you're lighter than me."

She did not argue. There was no time. She reached up for the rough wall top, and felt Dara heave from below. She came up through the glimmering sky-square, and went right over in a kind of swooping scramble, to land on the earth outside. There was a faint grunt and a scuffle, the dark shape of Dara's head and shoulders appeared through the hole, and next instant he had dropped on to his feet beside her.

She caught his hand, and began to run, out

toward the seaward side of the Dun, away from those terrible drums. When she pulled up, panting, they were at the gap in the turf walls where the stream gully passed through.

"Look! This is the way you must go—they don't guard this side. And when you're away, you'll be able to find a war band of your own people."

They had scrambled down the dry runnel-bed, right to the far edge of the gap, and the cliff plunged almost from their feet to the sea creaming among the rocks far below. Dara looked down—and down—and down—and swallowed as though he felt sick.

"You've got to go that way!" she whispered fiercely. "It's easy."

"If it's so easy, why don't they guard it?"

"Because the water from the spring makes it slippery, and no one could keep his footing on the wet rocks. But now it's dry. Don't you see? It's dry!" She fished hurriedly down the front of her tunic, and held something out to him. "Here's a barley cake. Now go quick!"

But the boy Dara hesitated an instant longer. "Nessan, why are you doing this?"

"I—don't want you to be killed."

"I don't want to be killed either. But Nessan, what will they do to you?"

"They will not do anything. No one will know that I had anything to do with it, if only you go quickly."

Dara tried to say something more, then flung an arm round her neck in a small fierce hug and next instant was creeping forward alone.

She was half crying, as he crouched and slithered away, feeling for every hand- and foothold along the grass-tufted cliff edge, and disappeared in the black moon-shadow of the turf wall. She waited, shivering, ears on the stretch for any sound. Once she heard the rattle of a falling pebble, but nothing more. At last she turned back toward the Chief's Hall, and the quickening throb of the wolfskin drums.

To Dara, that time of clinging and clambering along the shelving ledges of bare rocks and summer-burned grass, with the turf wall rising steeply on his right side, and on his left the empty air and the drop to the fanged rocks and the sea, was the longest that he had ever known. And at every racing heartbeat he was terrified of a false step that would send him whirling down into that dreadful emptiness with the rocks at the bottom of it, or betray him to the terrible little dark men within the Dun. But at last the space between the turf wall and cliff edge grew wider, and then wider still, and soon he was clear of the Dun, and the deserted turf huts scattered inland of it, and he gathered himself together and ran.

After a while he slowed down. No sense in simply running like a hare across country, and he had no idea in what direction he would find the war bands of his own people. And at that moment he realized that he had no weapon. Nessan had slipped her knife back into her belt after she had cut his bonds, and neither of them had thought of it again. He was alone and unarmed in an enemy country. Well, there was nothing to do but keep going and hope that he would not need to kill for food or run into any kind of trouble before he found his own people.

Presently, well into the hills, he came upon a moorland pool, where two streamlets met. It was so small and shallow that he could have waded through it in several places, and scarcely get wet to the knee. And the moon, still high in the glimmering sky, showed him an upright black stone that stood taller than a man, exactly between the two streamlets where they emptied themselves into the pool. A black stone, in a countryside where other stones were grey; and twisted about the narrowest part near the top, a withered garland of tough moorland flowers: ling and ragwort and white-plumed bog-grasses.

Dara stood staring at it with a feeling of awe. And as he did so, a little wind stirred the dry garland, and from something fastened among the brittle flowerheads, the moonlight struck out a tiny blaze of brilliant blue fire! Nessan's blue glass arm-ring! He caught his breath, realizing that this must be the Goddess herself, the Black Mother. But at the same instant, he noticed the spear which stood upright in the tail of the pool. A fine spear, its butt ending in a ball of enamelled bronze; an Irish spear!

His own people must have passed this way and come across the Goddess whose People they had been raiding, and left an offering to turn aside her anger. He noticed also that the spear, set up in what seemed to be the place where the two streams joined before the feet of the Black Mother, had caught a dead furze branch on its way down and twigs and birch leaves and clumps of dry grass, even the carcase of some small animal, had drifted into the furze branch and clung there, building up into something like a small beaver's dam, and blocking the stream so that it had spread out into a pool. And as the pool grew high enough, it had begun to spill over into a new runnel that it was cutting for itself down the hillside.

Dara was not interested in the changed course of a stream, but he needed that spear; needed it so badly that his need was greater even than his fear of taking it.

He caught a deep breath and turned to the tall garlanded stone that seemed to him now to stand like a queen in the moonlight. "Black Mother, do not be angry. I must have the spear. See, I will leave you a barley cake and my amber necklace instead. That is two gifts for one!"

And his heart racing, he stepped into the water and pulled up the spear. For a moment he expected the sky to fall on him or the hillside to open and close again over his head. But nothing happened, and he went on his way, following the faint track of the war band that he could pick up here and there by trampled grass or a thread of dark wool caught on a bramble spray, and the droppings left by driven cattle.

And behind him, now that the spear that had held it was gone, little by little the dam washed away, and the pool sank, as the water returned to its old stream bed and sang its way downhill, to disappear under a bramble bush in the place where it had always gone underground before the raider left his spear for the Black Mother.

And where it went from there, under the turf and the rocks and the hawthorn bushes on its way to the sea, was a secret that neither Dara nor the Irish raiders nor Nessan's People knew. Only the stream singing to itself in the dark, knew that secret.

At moon-set, when the drumming grew still, and the pine knot torches all round the space below the Chief's Hall began to flare more brightly in the dark time before the dawn, several warriors of the Chief's kin went to fetch Dara from his prison. They came running back shouting that the boy was gone!

The word ran like a squall of wind through the crowd, and the Chief sprang up from his seat of piled oxhides. "Gone?"

"There's not a sign of him—not a shadow."

"And his cut bonds lying beside the centre post, and the summer-strip turned back from the roof edge!"

The Chief turned upon the warrior who had guarded the door hole. "Istoreth, what do you say as to this?"

The warrior looked his Chief steadily in the eye, but in the light of the torches his face was ashy, for he knew what to expect. "I kept my watch. I saw nothing, I heard nothing," he said.

"Ill have you kept your watch! And the Black Mother waits for her sacrifice. If the boy is not found, then you must take his place. Is it fair and just?"

"It is fair and just," the man said.

The Chief turned from him to the warriors standing close around. "Go you and search all within the stockade—every corner, every hut."

But before they could move to obey him, Nessan, on the dark fringe of the crowd, heard her own voice, high and silvery and very clear, as though it were not hers at all but somebody else's, "You will not find him! He is not here!"

There was a sudden hush, everyone looked towards her, and in the hollow heart of the hush, the Chief her father demanded in a terrible voice, "Nessan, what thing have you done?"

Nessan walked forward into the torchlight, the people parting to let her through. "I helped him to escape, my Father, through the gap where the spring water goes. It is dry, not slippery, now that the water—does not run."

The Chief groaned and covered his face with his hands, and Laethrig the Priest, who had been standing by all this while, spoke for the first time. "And you are daring to come forth here and tell us of it?"

"Yes, Old Holy One." Nessan tried desperately to steady her voice.

"You are very brave, my child, or very foolish!"

Nessan drew a long shivering breath. "You cannot kill Istoreth. It was not his fault. I—I knew when I helped Dara away, that if the well did not fill again, I must come here instead of him."

"It is of your own choosing," said the old priest, very gently . "So be it, then; come here to me."

"No!" cried the Chief.

"Yes!" said the old priest, as gently as ever. He was holding the black pottery bowl that was used for only one thing, to hold the drink that brought the Long Sleep at the time of sacrifice.

Nessan took a step towards him, and wavered for a moment, then walked steadily forward.

Everything was very quiet, nobody moved or whispered in all the crowd; the only sound was the restless stirring of the thirsty cattle. And then into the quiet, there fell a tiny sound; a soft "plop" and then a faint trickling from the well that had been sullenly silent all night long.

"No, wait!" one of the women cried. "Listen!"

"What to, then?"

"There it is again!"

"It is the well! The spring is coming back to life!"

That time all those near enough to the spring heard it, and a great gasp went up from them. They crowded round the well-pool; then they were parting and pushing back to make a path for the Chief and Laethrig to pass through.

Nessan did not move. She stood where she was, and shut her eyes tight; she heard another plop and a wet green trickling, and the murmur of the crowd; and then her father crying out in a great triumphant voice, "The water is rising! You see, Old Holy One? You hear?"

"I see and I hear," said the old priest. "It is in my heart that the Black Mother is no longer angry with us. . . ."

And she knew from his voice that he had gone away small inside himself, so that if you looked into his eyes it would be like looking through the doorway of an empty hut.

Everyone waited, hearing the plop and ripple of the refilling well. And then at last Nessan heard the old man sigh, and the dry rustle of his necklaces, as he stirred and came back to himself. "The Black Mother has spoken to me. She calls for no more sacrifice in this matter; she says the willingness is enough—the willingness is enough."

Nessan opened her eyes, half dazzled for the moment by the flare of the torches, and saw the Chief her father coming towards her, and flung herself into his arms, crying partly for sorrow that Dara was gone, and partly with relief so that there was not enough room for it all inside her, and partly because she was suddenly more tired than she had ever been in all her life.

And the Chief picked her up and carried her away to her own sleeping-place in the women's hut behind the great Hall. She was asleep before he laid her down on the dappled deerskin rugs.

At the same time, far up in the hills, a broken curlew's feather, the very last that was left of the dam, shook itself clear of the bog-myrtle of the stream bank, and went eddying downstream.

THE WHITE HORSE

Ruth Ainsworth

A LITTLE BOY named Odd lived in a cottage on the
sea shore with his father and mother and his sister
Freda. The cottage was on the beach, with rocks
behind, and sand and shingle all around. The
children's feet were so tough from running about
without shoes that they could climb over the hard
rocks, and jump on the sharp pebbles, as easily as
on soft grass.

They had a garden in pots on the window sill,
where their mother grew flowers. The soil was
brought in a sack from inland and the seeds came
from a town many miles away.

Their father was a fisherman and Odd, when he
grew to be a man, would be a fisherman as well.

But he was too little to go to school, as yet. In a year or two, Freda and he would go by boat to the nearest school, but at present they did lessons with their mother, when she had time to teach them.

The beach was their garden, their playground and their nursery. Almost everything they played with, except Odd's wooden horse and Freda's doll, they found on the shore. They played shopping with shells and seaweed, and used pebbles for money. They made boats from driftwood and floated them in shallow pools.

When the storms came and the strong winds blew and the waves were high as houses, the children had to play indoors. But even in stormy weather Odd liked to put on his boots and thick scarf and his cap with ear-flaps, and go outside and watch the sea. When the waves broke with great, white, foaming crests and a sound like thunder, his father and mother said: "The white horses are out today." As he stood and watched, Odd thought the curling foam was just like the mane of a great white horse.

The children believed that every seventh wave was bigger than all the others, and they used to count them as they came swirling up the beach. When the seventh broke they shouted with joy and raced up and down. Foam blew into their faces and settled on the beach, and they called these fluffs "pancakes" and poked them with sticks, pretending to eat them.

Once, when Odd was on the beach alone, he thought he saw a real white horse rising out of the waves. He saw its head with a streaming white mane, and heard it snorting as it rose up, then plunged out of sight. The next evening, when darkness was falling, he saw its head even more plainly, and its delicate front feet pawing the water. He heard it neighing and saw its rolling dark eyes. Odd told no one about this wonderful horse except Freda, who listened, but said nothing. She was a silent child and used to listening to her brother's stories.

The next evening, at the same time, Odd saw the sea horse again, and this time it came riding in with the seventh wave and came right up the beach. It stood quietly beside Odd, hanging its head, and he put out his hand and patted the soft white nose which was damp, and yet warm. It neighed in a friendly way and then plunged back into the waves, leaving its hoof marks in the wet sand to be wiped away by the next wave.

Odd was so excited that he could not get to sleep. If he saw this wonderful horse again he decided he would fetch his father and mother to see the sight. He could hardly bear to wait for the next evening.

The evening came at last, and Odd stood on the beach in his knitted cap and boots, watching and waiting. At last, riding on a curling breaker, the sea horse came snorting and pawing on to the shore. Once again, Odd patted its nose as it stood beside him. He was hardly surprised when the horse spoke to him:

"Get on my back, Odd, and I will take you for a ride."

Odd hesitated, not quite knowing what to do.

"Wouldn't you like to have a ride?" asked the horse again. "Just a little one?"

"Yes," said Odd. "Yes, I would. I'll go and ask my mother."

He ran into the cottage and pulled his mother out by the hand.

"Look, mother, look!" he cried. But the sea horse had gone and a wave swept over the hoof marks before he could show them to her.

"I saw a great white horse—" he said.

"Yes," she replied calmly. "Yes, the white horses are out riding tonight," and she looked out to sea. Then she went back indoors, and though Odd waited till twilight fell, he saw only the foaming waves.

The next time Odd saw the horse he had made up his mind what to do. He patted the wet nose, and when the horse said softly:

"Come for a ride on my back," he knew what to say.

"Yes, I'd like to come, but I'll fetch Freda, my sister, first. May she have a ride too?"

"Freda is too small," said the horse. "She might fall off. You have a ride first."

It stood quietly on the beach, not tossing its head or stamping its hoofs. Odd found himself scrambling on to the wide, white back.

"Hold tight to my mane," it said, "and grip with your knees. You are quite safe."

Odd did what he was told and in a moment they were off, galloping along the beach, the wet sand spurting up and the salt spray from the waves stinging his cheeks. Up and down they went, up and down, and Odd felt he would like to go on riding for ever. Sometimes the horse went a little way into the sea, but always swerved back to the shore. Suddenly Odd saw a green wave, higher than all the others, rising up like the side of a mountain.

"The seventh wave!" he shouted, and the horse snorted and swung round and plunged into the sea. Odd kept his seat as they went down, down, down till they reached the sandy floor of the ocean, strewn with rocks and shells and seaweed, strange in shape and colour.

The horse galloped on till they came to a row of rocky caves, each with a sea horse stabled inside. One cave was empty, and this was the stable of Odd's horse. A group of children with crowns on their heads hurried to meet them, half running and half swimming.

When the children saw Odd they were overjoyed, and took his hands, and touched his clothes. They led him away in their midst, only stopping to pat the horse's nose and lay their cheeks against his.

The children led Odd to a large cave hung with shining ribbons of coloured seaweed. There, on two thrones made of mother-of-pearl, sat a King and a Queen, wearing crowns of amber.

"Here is a boy at last," cried the children. "Snowfire brought him to us on his back."

The King and the Queen were as pleased to welcome Odd as the princes and princesses had been. They told him again and again that he was as dear to them as their own sons, and that anything he wanted they would give him. Snowfire should be his own horse to ride whenever he wished.

Odd smiled and thanked them, and could not help feeling at home among such friendly people. The thought of riding Snowfire just when he wanted was specially exciting, and he could hardly wait to go back to the stables.

"Will you do something for us?" asked the Queen, gently, laying her hand on his arm.

"Yes, if I can," said Odd.

"Will you teach the princes and princesses how to write? We have no books in our kingdom under the sea, and we want to write the history of our lives. We live for many hundred of years, so we have much to write."

"I'll try," said Odd doubtfully. "Mother gives me lessons but she hasn't much time. I can only write very easy words with not many letters in them."

"That will do," said the King and Queen. "We

will write our history in short words. They will be much easier for people to read than long, difficult ones."

So every morning Odd chose a smooth stretch of sand and taught the children their letters, using pointed sticks for pencils. When they knew their letters they went on to learn easy words like "fish" and "sun" and "man".

Afterwards a mermaid with a shining green tail and golden hair gave Odd a lesson on the harp. Then all the children could amuse themselves and Odd ran to the stable to ride Snowfire. He soon learned to swim like the others, too, and could keep up with them in their games.

Sometimes Odd told the sea children stories he had heard when he lived on land, and he repeated poems and nursery rhymes. They liked to hear about sheep and geese and pigs, and children going to school. These things were ordinary to Odd, but strange and wonderful to them.

The sea children, in their turn, told him stories about fish with eyes like lamps, and oyster shells in which pearls were hidden. They told him, too, of treasure which had come from wrecked ships, chests of gold and silver, and caskets of jewels.

There were no clocks under the sea and time did not seem to matter. Whenever Odd began to think about his home, something or someone interrupted him. Snowfire was waiting for a ride, or one of the royal children showed him a treasure or a toy.

Odd became specially friendly with Hesper, one of the princes who appeared to be about his own age. His name had been chosen because it sounded like the whisper of waves breaking on the shore. They did everything together, riding and racing and playing, and the other children called them "the twins" because they were never apart.

One day, Hesper ran to Odd with something in his hand.

"Look!" he cried. "Something strange I've found!"

"It is a watch," said Odd, wondering how it had been lost and had sunk to the bottom of the sea. He had learned to tell the time just before he left home on Snowfire's back, and he saw that the hands had stopped at six o'clock. Six o'clock! That was the time when his mother took Freda on her lap and Odd sat on a stool at her feet, while she read to them. It was the part of the day he loved best of all, watching the flames leaping round the logs, and hearing his mother's voice going on and on. Suddenly he felt so homesick that he could hardly answer Hesper's questions about the watch, what it was for, whether it could be mended and made to tick again.

Odd went to the rocky stable where Snowfire stood, and stroked and patted him, but for once his friendly neigh and soft cheek were not comforting.

Several days went by, and though Odd taught

the sea children as usual, and had his own harp
lesson from the mermaid, his thoughts were some-
where else. He saw, in his mind, the little cottage
on the shore, and Freda in her blue jersey with her
fair pigtails bobbing as she skipped along. He gave
a start as he thought he heard his mother calling:
"Odd! Freda? Where are you? It's time to come
in".

He made up his mind to go home and to take
Hesper with him, if Hesper would come. When
he explained his plans, Hesper was eager to agree.

"Shall I see a sheep with wool all over it?"

"Yes."

"And a cat that says miaow?"

"Yes."

"And a hen that lays eggs for our breakfast?"

"Yes."

"Then I'll come."

They decided to leave that same evening, and
they slipped away to Snowfire's stable.

"Take me home to the land, Snowfire," said
Odd, as he mounted, and Hesper scrambled up
behind.

At once Snowfire rose through the clear green
water and came out among the rolling waves on
the surface. They plunged towards the shore,
sometimes riding on the crests of foam, sometimes under the water, and at last Odd caught a
glimpse of the rocky beach he knew so well, and
the chimney of the cottage.

As the boys dismounted on the wet sand, Snow-fire wheeled round, tossed his white head, and plunged under the waves, neighing good-bye.

They found Odd's father and mother and Freda having supper.

"You are late," said his father, "so we started without you."

"I couldn't find you anywhere," said Freda. "Where were you hiding? I had to come home alone."

Then Odd understood that his stay under the sea had seemed only a few minutes by clock time. He was welcomed and kissed, and Hesper was made much of like a son of the house.

"He is a prince," explained Odd, "and he's going to stay with us for a while. He can share my bed and play with us like a brother."

"Well," said his mother, "prince or no prince, he'll want his supper, and that's certain." She went to the cupboard to fetch an extra mug and bowl.

Odd was glad to have his own bowl of thick soup and his own mug of milk. Hesper was so overcome with the wonder of the cottage, simple and bare though it was, that he could hardly swallow for looking round and asking questions. The clock ticking on the wall—the cat asleep on the rug—the fire itself, crackling and blazing—all were marvellous, all were different.

Freda soon grew to love her new brother from the kingdom under the sea, and the three of them played as happily on the beach as Odd had played under the water. Hesper joined in the children's lessons and learned to write so well that he was sure that he would be able to write the history of his family when he went home. But he seldom spoke of going home, and every day he grew more and more like a land boy.

One thing he needed was a daily swim in the sea, and however wild the weather, and high the waves, he dived among them, disappearing for so long that Freda often began to cry. Then Hesper promised her he would never leave her without first saying good-bye, and this comforted her.

But the day came to Hesper, as it had come to Odd, when he was homesick. Winter came once more and the mountains were white with snow. The winds were cold and strong and the children had to play more often indoors. Hesper was happy enough all day, but at night, as he lay in bed with Odd beside him, he listened to the wind and the waves, and longed for home.

"I must go home," he said to Odd and Freda. "I must go home today." But that day there were sharp flurries of snow and the children were not allowed outside. The next day they managed to slip out after tea, as dusk was falling, for a breath of fresh air before bed-time.

"We want to see the white horses galloping," they said, as their mother tied their scarves round them, and pulled their caps over their ears.

The white horses were out, tossing their flowing manes, and soon the children caught a glimpse of Snowfire's head, and heard him snorting in the wind. Nearer and nearer he came, till a mighty wave, the seventh, brought him prancing to the shore.

Hesper climbed quickly on to his back, while Odd and Freda patted his nose and stroked him. Hesper bent down and held out his hand to Freda.

"Come too!" he begged. "Come for a visit to the kingdom under the sea!"

"No," said Odd, taking hold of Freda's coat. "No. She is too little. She must stay on land with her mother."

Freda held up her arms to Hesper, wanting to go with him. As their hands met, the cottage door opened and the children's mother called out:

"Come in, now. It's getting dark. Come in quickly."

Snowfire wheeled round and leapt among the waves and disappeared, but not before Freda had been dragged to the water's edge, gripped by Hesper.

When Odd and Freda were safe in the cottage, Freda was crying and Odd was pale and frightened. He described what had happened, and his mother took Freda on her lap and hugged her when she heard how nearly she had been snatched away.

"How glad the King and the Queen will be to have their own son back again," said the father and mother, wiping their eyes because they felt they had lost a son themselves. "Families must live together."

The children never saw Hesper again, but when the sea was rough and the white horses were out, Snowfire often came to greet them. He neighed with pleasure when he was stroked and patted. But when he said: "Come for a ride on my back!" the children shook their heads.

THE BEST SHOES BROGEEN EVER MADE

Patricia Lynch

BROGEEN THE LEPRECHAUN was sitting on his three-legged stool under the giant beech tree at the top of the Boreen of the Stepping Stones. He had brought his work table out into the sunshine and was putting the last touches to a pair of dancing shoes he was making for the Queen of *Tir-na-nOg*. It was Midsummer Eve and Brogeen wanted her to have them in good time for the great feast that always was held in the Fairy Fort under Slieve Mish mountain.

"I'll have to tidy meself up a bit," he muttered. "There's me green cloak and the goldy-brown sandals and me new belt. Pon me word, I'd like to be a credit to the boreen!"

Trud, the little elephant, who was the leprechaun's faithful companion, was standing on the bank of the stream, contentedly chewing a patch of long grass.

"Hi, you!" called Brogeen. "Give yourself a bit of a wash. We're going over yonder tonight and I'll not want to be disgraced before me old friends. That crusty Doorkeeper will have a few words to say if we go there looking like two old ones from the Back of Beyond!"

Trud replied by squirting a trunkful of water over himself and then rolling over at the bottom of the tiny waterfall.

"Will ye look at him!" grumbled the leprechaun. "I've a mind not to be taking him with me at all!"

In spite of Trud's splashing, he heard his master's voice and came stumping back on to the bank, giving his floppy ears a shake that sent a shower of water over the leprechaun.

Brogeen didn't mind being drenched, for the evening was hot, but he feared for those lovely shoes. He sprang to his feet in a fury, seized a lump of rock lying on the ground and flung it at the little elephant.

Trud saw the rock coming and flopped into the stream so that it passed harmlessly over him. The leprechaun reached out for another piece of rock. But he noticed that the shoes had escaped damage. There wasn't a spot of water on them.

"Thanks be!" he exclaimed and sat there admiring his wonderful work and, of course, admiring himself still more.

"Whisha! I'm stiff and tired!" he sighed, suddenly realizing that he had been crouching over his work for hours and had forgotten all about eating and drinking.

His fire was out, his kettle empty and there was only the heel of a stale loaf in the cupboard.

"There'll be plenty to eat when I arrive at the Fort," he told himself. "But when will that be?"

Tears of self-pity gathered in his eyes. He sat in a forlorn heap, not wanting to move, longing for a cup of tea and something—anything—to eat.

"Master!" called Trud. "Master! Will ye look what's coming?"

"Quit bothering me!" snapped Brogeen. "I'm wore out and I don't want to be vexed with your old chat."

Two voices called together, "Brogeen! Brogeen! See what we've brought you."

Brogeen looked up but the sunlight was so strong that he had to shade his eyes with his hand before he could see the two children, Judy and Jim MacDonald, who lived in a cabin on the mountainside, coming down the path towards him. They walked carefully for, between them, they carried a heavy basket and Jim held a tin jug with a lid.

" 'Pon my word!" chuckled Brogeen. "If they're

bringing what I think they are, me troubles are pretty well over."

He longed to run across the stepping stones to meet them but was too proud to show how delighted he felt.

The brother and sister stopped at the edge of the stream. Jim drew a deep breath.

"Me mother told me to say—Here's something for you with her best wishes and she hopes the work goes well!"

"And you're not to bother about washing dishes or anything like that," added Judy.

"Oh, Brogeen!" she cried suddenly, pointing at the shoes he was holding. "You've finished them. How lovely they are!"

If Brogeen had been pleased when he saw the well-filled basket, now he was delighted. Praise of his work meant more to him than food or drink. He was no longer tired but felt strong and clever.

He laid the shoes carefully on his little table.

"They are grand!" agreed Jim. "You must be the best shoe-maker in all Ireland!"

Brogeen settled himself comfortably and smiled at the children.

"Give your mother me best thanks!" he said. "Wait now, I'll unpack the basket and you can take it back. I haven't had a minute to spare. Me cupboard's empty and the fire is out."

"Fix everything up tomorrow," Jim told him. They unpacked the basket and soon the table was piled with all Mrs. MacDonald had sent—a big soda cake, a meat pie with baked potatoes so well wrapped they were still piping hot, a baked rice pudding in a dish and a thick slice of currant cake as well as the jug of tea with milk and sugar in it.

Brogeen's eyes opened wider and wider. When the basket was empty he stood scratching his head.

"Now how will I send back the pie dish?" he wanted to know. "Twill need a bit of cleaning, even when I've scraped it."

"Me mother said to bring back the basket but not to bother about the dish. She said you could put it in the stream to soak and we'll collect it next time we're passing. Good-bye!"

Jim grabbed the empty basket and off they ran.

It wasn't long before Brogeen had the fire alight. He took in the table and the stool, settled himself comfortably and soon was busy filling his mouth with meat, gravy and pie-crust.

Trud had wandered off while Brogeen was talking to the children. Now he thrust his head in at the door.

"Master!" he grunted gently. "Would there be ere a scrap or two left over for me? That meat pudden smells grand and I'm sick and tired of grass and twigs, wid not a tasty bite in the lot."

Brogeen had, without being asked, saved the hardest bits of pie-crust for Trud. But he pretended to be scandalized at such a demand.

"'Pon me word!" he cried. "Ye have the whole mountainside covered wid good eating and you have to come wanting the food the kind woman up the mountain sent to save me from starvation!"

Trud heaved a deep sigh.

"I s'pose ye have the rights of it," he said mournfully. "But the smell has me longing."

The little elephant was turning away when Brogeen heaped the bits of pie-crust on the ground before him.

"There y'are, ye eejit!" he chuckled. "Have I ever grudged you the bits of left-overs, have I now?"

Trud was too busy crunching and gulping to make any answer.

"As soon as I'm rested I must give meself a tidy-up to be ready for the goings-on at Slieve Mish," said Brogeen, stretching his legs before him.

"Thanks be, I've had a grand wash in the stream," grunted Trud. "I wouldn't want ye to be ashamed of me before them all!"

"Who do you think will look twice at you in the Fort," retorted Brogeen indignantly. "They've seen a bit more than the simple people in these parts, let me tell you!"

Trud stood up and glared at his master.

"They've never seen the likes of me!" he declared proudly.

Brogeen opened his mouth to say something

very scornful. He closed it again for he began to think that Trud was quite right.

"Ah well," he muttered. "'Twill do no harm if we both do ourselves up as grand as we can. I'll get out me best suit and me new red cap, and I'll give me shoes a polish."

At last the leprechaun was ready and he looked so smart he was sorry Jim and Judy weren't there to see him when he rode off on Trud's back. Still, all the blackbirds, the thrushes, the hedge sparrows, the squirrels, the moles and field mice of the neighbourhood were there, and they made such an uproar that Brogeen longed to stop and make them a speech of farewell. Yet he knew he should be on his way, so he smiled, waved his hand and started to scold Trud.

"Stir yer stumps, will ye?" he snapped. "Do ye want us to be the last of the guests to arrive? I want to be there first to give Her Majesty the shoes I've made."

He slapped the neat little parcel he carried under his arm.

"And I never set eyes on a grander pair, master," said the little elephant. "If the Queen isn't crazy wid joy I'll be amazed!" Brogeen was so pleased at this praise that he didn't say another word to Trud until they had crossed the river by the Bridge of the Seven Arches and were through the market town on the other side. Then he saw that the shadows were growing longer and longer.

"What ailed me not to start with the dawn," he grumbled. "I'd love to see all the other ones arriving! Stir yer stumps, Trud, and don't be stopping at every twist and turn of the road!"

"What about going up aloft for a bit?" suggested Trud. "We'd be twice as quick that way."

Brogeen considered this.

"No!" he decided, "I don't want the world to know where I'm going. I like me comings and goings to be me own business once in a while."

Trud marched on. They came to a mossy bank above the river. The sun made a golden path over the water where swans were gliding gracefully, gazing proudly at their reflections.

Trud stopped. He was breathless for Brogeen had been urging him to trot his fastest. The leprechaun slipped to the ground. For once he did not grumble. He settled himself in a sunny corner and unwrapped the parcel he was carrying.

Brogeen held up the shoes he had made for the Queen of *Tir-na-nOg*. The silver and gold threads on the green velvet sparkled like jewels.

"'Pon me word, I've never done a better bit of work!" Brogeen told himself proudly. "There'll not be a finer pair of shoes throughout the length and breadth of the Hidden Kingdom, that's sure! Herself will be pleased—no doubt of that! But there's something wrong, something missing! What can it be?"

"What a sight for tired eyes!" said a voice above him—a sweet, sad voice.

He started and looked up. The oldest, poorest-looking woman he had ever seen was standing before him. She clasped her thin hands tightly as she gazed in wonder at the shoes.

"I've never seen more beautiful work," she sighed. "The one who made them must be the cleverest shoe-maker in Ireland!"

Brogeen's cheeks grew red.

"Thank ye kindly, ma'am!" he muttered. "I was thinking to meself—they're the best shoes I ever made!"

The old woman sat beside him.

"You should be famous!" she told him. "What name is on you, great shoe-maker? I suppose you did make them yourself?"

"Of course I made them!" exclaimed the little leprechaun. "And the name on me is *Brogeen*."

He spoke so proudly even Trud was impressed.

The old woman looked from Brogeen to the shoes and back again. Her eyes opened wider and wider.

"Brogeen!" she whispered. "I've heard of you—Brogeen of the Stepping Stones, who makes shoes for the Little People. You are famous!"

Brogeen swelled with pride.

The old woman smiled and nodded.

"And who is the lucky one who will wear those shoes?"

"*Herself!*" said the little shoe-maker. "The Queen of *Tir-na-nOg*. She'll wear them tonight, on Midsummer Eve, at the Ball inside Slieve Mish. I'm on me way to present them now—"

The old woman touched the shoe nearest her with a thin, bony finger.

"Such embroidery," she sighed. "Rosebuds and purple pansies, ferns, and a golden butterfly on each toe. And look at the heels! Who could help but dance like a fairy in such shoes. Once I could dance. But look at the shoes I wear now. Wouldn't you pity me?"

She stretched out her feet and both the leprechaun and Trud gazed at the broken, shapeless shoes she wore.

She kicked them off and, if her shoes were shapeless, her bare feet were lovely—smooth, small, white, with pink nails like shells.

She looked pleadingly at Brogeen.

"If only I could slip my feet into these beautiful shoes, just to know what they would feel like. May I, Master Shoe-maker? Surely your Queen wouldn't grudge a poor old woman a moment's happiness?"

Brogeen hesitated but she snatched the shoes from him and slipped them on her feet. As he put out his hand to stop her, she danced away—away! The road she took turned sharply by a giant oak and, though they ran their hardest, when they reached it she had disappeared.

"Wirra! Wirra!" Brogeen lamented, shaking his head. "What will I do at all! We'd best turn round and go back the way we came. How can I ever show my face at the Fort and me empty-handed!"

Trud was sorry for him.

"Let's go up aloft!" he urged. "We'll see which way she's gone and we can lep down on her."

" 'Pon my word, ye have the rights of it!" exclaimed Brogeen. "Up and off wid us!"

He jumped on Trud's back and Trud leaped into the air.

Up! Up! Up! they went into the wind and the sunshine. The countryside lay below them, like a giant painting—hedges, ditches, woods where the smaller trees were crowded together and the great trees stood alone. There were grand houses with high walls, cabins with golden thatched roofs scattered over the brown bog; villages where the houses clustered together, chapels with pointed spires and square-built schoolhouses. Carts and motor cars were coming and going on the roads like tiny toys; meek little donkeys were drawing heavy burdens, children played on the greens and in the narrow streets.

They saw all they expected to see. But there was never a sign of the tall, thin, ragged woman who had stolen the dancing shoes.

"If this doesn't beat all," groaned the leprechaun. "Where in the wide world can she have got to?"

He gave Trud a slap.

"Get along out of this," he ordered. "It only makes me mad to see all I know must be there but never a glimpse of what I want to see. Get down!"

Trud obeyed, not without grumbling.

"Quit chattering and do as ye're bid!" ordered Brogeen.

Trud landed with a bump.

"Now I've to climb the mountain," he complained. "Why couldn't we have kept on till we were at the top?"

"So that old doorkeeper could see us coming and get a great laugh. No, me bold boyo! I'll take him by surprise and before he knows who or what we are, we'll be inside."

"Ye'll not take that one by surprise," said Trud. "Ye should know that as well as I do, master."

Brogeen gave him another slap and they went on in silence.

"I wonder am I wise not to go back home," mused the little shoe-maker. "Here was I all set up with the lovely shoes, letting this one and that one know what I was doing. And here am I now— empty handed!"

He heaved such a deep sorrowful sigh that Trud looked at him with sympathy.

"Is it them dratted shoes has ye flummoxed, master?" he asked gently.

Brogeen nodded.

"It is indeed! The shoes I put me best work into and now I've nothing to show for me labours!"

Trud stopped so suddenly that Brogeen cried out indignantly.

"Will ye look where ye're going! Ye great big lumbering eejit!" he cried.

"Listen!" grunted Trud. "Yer troubles is over and ended!"

"They are! Are they?" jeered Brogeen. "That's great news—if true!"

"True indeed!" exclaimed the little elephant. "Didn't I hear ye say—the best part of them shoes was the buckles? And I wondered why ye didn't sew them on. But I know how contrary ye can be so I kept me mouth shut. I thought mebbe ye had a notion to give Her Majesty the shoes. Then, when she was dancing round in delight, ye'd bring out the buckles and hand them over, so that she'd have another present and everyone in *Tir-na-nOg* would think ye a bigger wonder than ever. Well, ye have the buckles unless ye forgot all about them and left them behind!"

Trud stood with his head on one side and his ears standing up straight, not sure whether Brogeen would be pleased or angry.

Brogeen stared at his companion. A smile spread slowly over his face.

He opened his little bag, drew out the buckles and held them up so that the sunlight shone down on them and they gleamed like crushed rainbows.

"Up and off with you!" he ordered. "What do I care about the shoes now I have the buckles!"

Trud leapt into the air joyfully and up they went.

Brogeen had forgotten what a crowd gathered at Slieve Mish for the Midsummer Eve Ball. He thought they would arrive by themselves but here were the jostling crowds of the Secret World. Only for Trud it might have happened that he would have given up the struggle to enter in disgust. But the little elephant, his master on his back, gave a leap into the air and came down at the entrance itself, landing almost on top of the Guardian of the Door.

"How dar ye? How dar ye?" screamed the cross little doorkeeper. "Stand back there! Get into line and take your turn."

But, by now, Brogeen and Trud were inside, pushing and squeezing through the crowd of Little People till they reached the Banqueting Hall where the guests were just beginning to take their seats at the long tables.

There were so many leprechauns and cluricauns, as well as horned women and other queer guests, that Brogeen was glad to have the little elephant close beside him. He had been so long away from the Fort that they seemed strange.

"Sit down here by me," said a friendly voice. "I want to hear all your adventures in the world outside."

Brogeen put his elbows on the table and opened his mouth to begin the story of his adventures but there was the Chief Harper of the Fort, taking his seat on the wide steps below the throne, while two little cluricauns put his harp down beside him.

"Wait till the old lad's finished," whispered his neighbour. "I'd never want to miss a note of his playing."

"Nor me!" agreed Brogeen.

As he listened, sipping at a goblet of golden wine, he looked about him at the magnificent scene which he had not set eyes on for so long.

The high roof and the walls glittered as if made of jewels. The hangings were woven of rich silks—crimson, green, gold, blue. The tables and benches along the walls were so exquisitely carved he longed to follow the tracing with the tips of his fingers.

From every arch hung lanterns, so that there were few dark spots. The centre of the floor was crowded with dancers.

Dignified wolfhounds and timid unicorns moved in and out the tables, taking titbits from the feasters. White cats lay on silk cushions spread for their comfort.

The King and Queen sat at the far end of the hall, dining at a golden table. The Queen looked over the Chief Harper's head and saw Brogeen. He found himself looking straight into her eyes and wondered how he could have stayed away so long.

"Welcome home, Brogeen!" she called. "I began to think you had gone from us for ever. Come nearer! I must talk to you!"

The leprechaun felt his ears tingling as he trotted down the hall with Trud lumbering at his heels.

"Sure, I wouldn't do that, Your Majesty!" he said. "You might know I'd always come back!"

"How could I be sure?" she asked sadly. "If you didn't seem to know or care if I had shoes to dance in."

Trud put up his trunk and bellowed. He had meant to whisper but he was better at making a noise. This time he made such a racket the musicians stopped playing, the dancers stood still and the King woke up from the nap he was taking.

"What's happened?" he cried, looking round, "What's wrong?"

He looked at Brogeen.

"It's you, is it?" he snapped. "They would blow the trumpets and beat the drums to let us know you're here. I suppose we should be thankful if we see you once in a hundred years. Well, now you're here what have you to say for yourself? Did you bring Her Majesty a new pair of shoes?"

There wasn't a sound in the Fort. Everyone was wondering what Brogeen would say for they could see his hands were empty. Trud scuffled and grunted

"Tell that ugly beast of yours to keep quiet," ordered the King.

"Sh!" said the Queen. "I think dear little Trud is trying to give Brogeen some good advice."

"Pity he didn't start sooner," grumbled the King.

Brogeen looked thoughtful.

"Trud's right," he muttered. "Doesn't happen often! But there's nothing else for it but to tell Herself the whole story."

"'Twas this way, Your Majesty," he began meekly. "I was making a pair of dancing shoes for you. They had high heels, pointed toes and every scrap of them was embroidered with rosebuds and purple pansies, with a golden butterfly on each toe. Best of all I had a pair of buckles, gold they were, studded with diamonds, rubies and pearls. I didn't put the buckles on because I was afraid they might get a knock. I kept them in me pocket."

"Very sensible," muttered the King. "Very sensible indeed!"

"On the way I took out the shoes, meaning to fix the buckles before I presented them to Your Majesty, when a beggar woman came along and stole them off me."

"Oh, Brogeen—how shocking!" cried the Queen. "How shall we punish her?"

"Leave her be—if we get back the shoes!" said Brogeen.

He looked sadly at the Queen, who was sitting up very straight and dignified but with a mischievous twinkle in her eyes.

"It makes me angry to think of those beautiful shoes on a beggar woman's big, ugly feet," she said.

Brogeen shook his head.

"Her feet weren't ugly, or big either," he protested. "They were smooth and white, and the nails were like pink shells."

"You felt sorry for her, Brogeen?" asked the Queen softly.

He nodded.

"Were her feet more beautiful than mine?" she persisted. "Perhaps I should take off my shoes so that you can see them."

She put out her feet. Brogeen stared, unable to believe his eyes, for the shoes the Queen was wearing were those which he had made with such care and pride—the shoes which the strange woman had stolen from him.

The Queen pulled them off and, with them, her golden gossamer stockings. Brogeen thought her feet looked even lovelier than when she had pretended to be a poor beggar woman.

"Very pretty! Very pretty!" said the King. "What a shame Brogeen didn't put on the buckles."

"I have them here!" declared Brogeen proudly, bringing them out.

The King cried out in admiration. So did the Queen and so did everyone else in the great hall while Trud trumpeted joyfully. Brogeen took the buckles and slapped them on to the shoes where they stuck as if they were glued there.

"So you were that bold beggar woman," said the King, turning to the Queen. "Whatever made you get up to such shocking antics?"

The Queen laughed.

"I knew where Brogeen lived and I set off to meet him for I was sure he would be on his way here for Midsummer Eve. I dressed myself like a beggar woman and set out on the journey. There he was taking his ease with his baby elephant, holding up the shoes, admiring his own work. I thought it would be great fun to get them away from him, and it was!"

"I'm surprised at you!" declared the King sternly.

"Are you?" asked the Queen, her head on one side, her eyes dancing.

The King rubbed his chin and chuckled.

"Well, now you've had your fun, how are you going to thank Brogeen for the lovely shoes and the grand buckles? How will you make up for all the annoyance you've given him?"

The Queen looked at Brogeen. Brogeen looked at the Queen.

"Sure," he mumbled, "I'm not annoyed. How could I be? I've never seen a pair of my shoes look grander. But if Herself would give me a bit of a dance, I'd be the proudest leprechaun in all Ireland!"

Without a word the Queen jumped down to the floor of the great hall and held out her arms.

And there was Brogeen the leprechaun, along with the Queen, leading the dance and, though his head didn't come up to her shoulder, there wasn't one in the Banqueting Hall of Slieve Mish who had ever seen such dancing.

THE FROG AND THE OX

Ian Serraillier

Aloud, for group with percussion:
scraper, maraccas, cymbals, drum,
tambourine, triangle, swanee whistle,
bicycle pump, or whatever's handy.
Make up your own accompaniment.

Two frogs
Sat croaking down a country lane
A plop-song with a croak refrain,
When—heavy, heedless how he came
Or where he trod—an ox swung by.

One frog
Sat croaking down a country lane
A sad and lonely strain.

Mother Frog,
Splashing in her pool nearby,
Heard his piping piteous cry:

"Oh, mother, dear mother,
A dreadful beast obscured the sky.
His careless hoof crushed my brother
And trampled him in the mud, a-smother.
Oh, hurry, hurry!"

Two splashes—three hops—
She leaps through the air and plops beside him,
All froth and flurry:

"If you'd stayed at home, as you were told,
Under the lush marsh-marigold—
But what was he like, my dear? Describe him.
What was he like?"

"Four-legged he walked, with swishing tail and
    chewing chops
And magisterial slow mud-sucking pops—
Enormous."

"Like this?"

She puffed her portly figure
Into a speckled ball.

"Oh, bigger. A speckled ball
Is far too small.
Much bigger."

She puffed and puffed her portly figure
Into a green balloon.

"Oh, bigger. The sight would make you swoon.
Like Mars, Uranus or the Moon—
Much bigger."

"Like this?"

She puffed and puffed and puffed her portly figure
Into a monster pumpkin, red as fire.

"Oh, bigger, fuller, broader, higher,
Thick as a barn and tall as a spire.
MUCH bigger."

"Like this?"

With blow and bluster, vim and verve and vigour,
She puffed and puffed and puffed
    And puffed and puffed and puffed
    And puffed and puffed and puffed
        Her portly figure,
            Till
        (Come what must)
        She B-U-S-T!

RAINBOW

William Mayne

"WE WILL GO into the biggest café," said Berno. "It will make us bold."

"I do not want to be bold," said Marija. "I want to drink milk, not coffee."

"You may drink anything you like," said Berno. He led her among the tables that stood on the wide pavement. They sat down under a coloured umbrella. Marija smoothed her skirt over her knees and looked at Berno. He was blinking in the sun. He was not under the umbrella.

They had come down from Spolet, their own village, on one tram, and soon they had to take another, from the street outside this café, and go up to the castle.

"We have plenty of time," said Berno. "Plenty of time."

"Then why do you look at all the clocks every minute?" said Marija.

"I am nervous," said Berno. "My thoughts are jumping about inside me like a pebble in a balloon; I have to read all the clocks, because I dare not believe only one. If we were late for my appointment I should not get the job."

Marija wondered a little bit. She wondered why Berno should be nervous. He was twenty years old, twice her age. They had had three birthdays between them this year, one each on the right day, and a third one half-way between, when Marija came up to being exactly half Berno's age.

"I am glad you are with me," said Berno. "I should be even more nervous if I came by myself."

A waiter came out to them, and stood in his white coat in the sunshine. Berno had to close his eyes until Marija could not see what colour they were. She knew they were brown.

They drank their coffee and their milk. Then they crossed the pavement and waited for the tram that would take them up to the castle. It was always best to go on a tram, because the streets of the town were steep. There were no flat places in the part of the country where they lived. It was all mountains, all up or down and never level. The biggest flat place for miles around was the ball-room floor of the castle. Marija had seen it once.

The tram came grinding up the street. Its wheels grated and rang on the rails. Under the road there was a whirring, because there was a cable to help the tram come up. Berno got into the second car of the tram. The first one was full of people smoking.

"The smell of tobacco would choke me today," said Berno.

"It is better in the second car," said Marija. "We can look from the back window at the town."

Berno sat on the back seat with her. Most of the way up the hill to the castle there was a big wagon just behind, and that was all they could see: the driver and his mate, and the radiator making the air above it ripple with heat. Then the wagon went past, and they could see the town below, and the mountains beyond.

"There is Spolet," said Berno, pointing over to the left. "But our house is one of so many that I can't tell which it is. And over there, to the right, is Naznir, where Mother was born. See how the mountain sits between them. The only place Daddy and Mother could meet was here in the town."

"Perhaps they met in the café we went to," said Marija.

"Perhaps," said Berno. "But we were pretending to be rich this morning."

The tram went into a shadow. The shadow was the shadow of the castle. Berno stood up and bumped his head on the luggage rack.

"No hurry," said the conductor.

"I am nervous," said Berno. "I am going for a job with one of the professors here."

"Banging your head like that will not make you any cleverer," said the conductor. "Now wait until we stop, or you will bang it again, and break the safety law as well."

When the ground stopped moving beside them Berno got off, and helped Marija down the step. The tram rang a bell and went farther up the hill. It had a long way to go yet before it came back.

The doorway of the castle was big. It was shady inside like a cave. People were walking about inside. Berno looked round to see where he should go. In the end he had to ask a porter, who told him to go up the stairs at the end of the hall, and into a waiting-room there.

"What do they do here?" said Marija, when they were walking towards the stairs.

"Learning and teaching," said Berno. "I have learnt, and now it is time for me to learn again; but of course I must have a job from the professor so that I have enough money to live on. I am not a clever student and I did not win an award."

Up the stairs there was more light, because there was a long passage with windows in it all the way, looking out to the north.

"There is Spolet again," said Berno, looking out. "And Naznir."

The waiting-room was at the end of the passage. Berno and Marija went in and sat down.

"Perhaps I am late," said Berno. "No one has
come to me."

"There is a bell," said Marija. "You should
ring it, and they would know you are here."

The bell was on a table by the door. It said
beside it, "Ring for attention". Berno rang it.

"A good start," he said. "I did not see it. I am
glad you came, Marija. I might have sat here until
midnight."

When the bell rang another door opened and a
man looked out. Berno went over to him, and said
who he was, Berno Firovich. The man took him
into the room beyond the door, and Marija could
hear their voices talking quietly together. She sat
on the leather chair and looked round the room. It
was a room with no straight sides. It was a round
room. She thought it might be in one of the
towers of the castle. There were windows all along
half the curving wall, looking out over Spolet, and
right round to the east, to where the vineyards
came close against the castle. It was very quiet in
here. Marija could hear the leather chair creak as
she breathed.

She waited. The door opened again, and Berno
came out. After him came the man who had let
him in. They both came into the room. He looked
at Marija, as if he thought she had come for a job
too.

"It is my sister," said Berno. "There is a school
holiday just now. Marija, this is Professor Fendor."

Marija stood up and curtseyed, because professors are important men.

"Thank you," said the professor. "My students are not so polite. Have you enjoyed sitting in this room?"

"Yes, thank you, sir," said Marija.

"It is the room where Karistan was born," said the professor. "In this very room he drew his first breath. You know about Karistan, Marija?"

"Yes, sir," said Marija. "1582 to 1626. He was the son of Prince Slavedsky and Princess Theodora. In 1602 he freed the people of the land from the Turks and established a republic, which lasted after his death until the Turks overwhelmed the country again."

"You say it exactly like a book," said the professor. "You have learnt it in school, I can tell."

"Yes, sir," said Marija. She hoped she had said the right things to the professor. He seemed to be laughing at her a little. Now he spoke again.

"He was born in this very room," he said. "He was the father of freedom. It is said that Slavedsky, his father, looked from this window at the very moment he was born, and saw the famous rainbow standing in one of the villages, and he took that for a fortunate sign. No one knows which village it was, because Spolet and Naznir both claim it. But, whichever one it was, they say it was there that Karistan first began the revolt against the Turks. He was only a week old when the Turks took the castle and his parents had to leave the country. But he came back." The professor led them to the window. "There is Spolet, and there is Naznir," he said. "You can see them both from here. But which is the one where the freedom began?"

"Spolet," said Marija. "That is what we say. That is where we come from."

"But you do not *know*," said the professor. "It is not possible to say anything until you *know*. Is that not true, Firovich?"

"Yes, sir," said Berno.

"I shall be glad to *know*, whenever you find out, Marija," said the professor. "And I shall write to you, Firovich, very soon. Good-bye."

The professor went out of the room again, and Marija curtseyed again. "Now," she said, "did he give you the job?"

"I do not know," said Berno. "He has other students to see as well. He will not choose until he has seen them all. So I am waiting once more. Perhaps I shall never be a student again."

They went quietly back home. They caught the same tram going down as they caught coming up. "Was your head clear?" said the conductor.

"I do not know yet," said Berno. "I cannot tell."

At home the house was softly dark behind its shutters. Marija made some dinner for both of them, and they ate it in the shady garden under the vines. Then Berno went out again to see his friends and tell them how he had got on. Marija went to the bottom of the garden and on to the path beside the river to see who there was to play with. She found Elena, and they skipped along the edge of the river until Elena's mother called them in to drink tea.

They drank their tea indoors, with the shutters closed. The sunlight came in through the round ventilation holes in the shutters and made tunnels of light across the room. The steam of the tea rose into the light, and became brightly coloured, twinkling with red and blue and green.

"The colour is coming out of the tea," said Marija. "I can see it in the light."

"It is a rainbow," said Elena's father. "I see many rainbows. I see them in steam, I see them in water, I see them in snow and ice. I see them in rivers and on the waves and under the trees. You could see them if you were looking."

Marija thought she could not see them in so many places. But Elena's father had been in many places. He had been a sailor, climbing up the masts of sailing ships. Now he was a fireman, climbing tall ladders to rescue people. Marija blew the coloured steam away and said, "It is all rainbows today for me. But I only saw one, in your tea. I was talking to a professor this morning." She thought that would sound important to Elena and her family, but they knew about Berno's visit to the castle.

"Did he get the job?" said Elena's father.

"He does not know yet," said Marija.

"We hope he does," said Elena's father. "But we cannot help."

"The professor was talking about rainbows," said Marija. "Karistan's room is his waiting-room."

"It is time the castle was a museum, not a university," said Elena's father. "There should be No Smoking in there. Even our longest ladders could not rescue a burning professor from one of those high towers. But which village did Karistan's father see the rainbow in, Marija?"

"He does not know," said Marija. "He would like to know. He says it is not possible to say anything until you *know*."

"You hear that, love," said Elena's father to her mother. "You must not speak until you *know*. A professor has said so. Now you must believe it." He brushed his moustache on to his cheeks and laughed aloud. He thought he had made a good joke. "We could show him rainbows," he said. "We make fine ones in the brigade. The water shoots up from the hoses, and comes down again like rain, and rainbows are only rain and sun. On any fine day we can make them. I dare say that is what happened, and there was a fountain in Spolet with the sun shining on the water. That is what Slavedsky saw. It would be in the morning, when the sun is behind the castle."

"If Berno gets the job I will ask him to tell the professor that we have an idea," said Marija.

"We can do better than that," said Elena's father. "We can make him a rainbow. There is all the water in the world in the mountain, and no one is having a fire now. I will call out the brigade in the morning and make them practise in the village square. We will send up a fountain of our own, and the professor can look from his window and see it. Then he will know. And Naznir can no longer say that freedom began there. It began in Spolet."

"Of course it did," said Marija. "Where else did anything begin? But Mother comes from Naznir. How will she like it?"

"Truth is truth," said Elena's father. "We will practise in the morning."

"Who will tell the professor?" said Marija. "Shall I go on the tram to the castle and make him look from his window?"

"At what time?" said Elena's father. "There is a time for rainbows, and a time for no rainbows. When the sun is behind the castle. I will send Elena to tell you in the morning."

Berno came in after Marija had gone to bed, so she did not tell him about the rainbow. In the morning she thought she would leave it to be a surprise for him. Mother and Daddy went out to their work, and Berno took out his books and sat in the morning sun to work.

"Where are you going, Marija?" he said.

"Out to play," said Marija. "I will tell you something when I come back."

"Be good and quiet, then," said Berno. "I have this work to do."

"I will not disturb you," said Marija. She stayed near the house until Elena came running in.

"It is ten o'clock," said Elena. "Ten o'clock."

"It is not," said Berno. "It is half past eight."

"Something else is ten o'clock," said Marija. "Something will happen at ten o'clock. The fire-brigade will be in the square, making a fountain."

"Keep yourselves dry," said Berno.

Marija and Elena caught the tram at nine. They often went down into the town together. They sat at the back of the tram, and watched the rails sliding out behind it, as if the tram were laying them down.

They caught the second tram at the same place as yesterday, but without calling at the biggest café for coffee. They smelt the coffee, though, and saw the thick creamy cakes in the window. But they had only money for the tram fare.

The tram rattled up the hill to the castle and stopped. They got out, and Elena looked round her, rather like Berno the day before.

"This way," said Marija. "I was here yesterday."

The porter came out of his doorway and said, "Where are you children going? You can't come in here."

"We are going to see Professor Fendor," said Marija.

"Have you an appointment?" said the porter.

"No," said Marija. "We shall ring the bell in the waiting-room where Karistan was born."

"Wait a minute," said the porter. "You can't go in there without an appointment. I'll ring him up and see what he says. What's your name?"

"Firovich," said Marija. "And this is my friend."

The porter picked up his telephone, and spoke into it. Marija and Elena waited in the big porch with the warm air moving in and out over their heads. The porter put the telephone down and came out again.

"You can go up," he said. "You know where to go?"

Marija led the way. The hall seemed longer today than it had yesterday, and so did the passage to the waiting room. Inside the waiting-room the professor was waiting. Marija was disappointed, because she had wanted to ring the bell.

"Firovich?" said the professor. Marija curtseyed and after a moment so did Elena. The professor was looking for someone else, they thought. He was looking for Berno. "Where is he?" he asked.

"We came alone," said Marija. "Berno is studying."

"I am glad to hear it," said the professor. "I told him I should write to him."

"It is not about that," said Marija. "It is about Karistan. If you look out of the window at Spolet when it is ten o'clock, you will see a rainbow."

"Indeed," said the professor, looking at his watch, and putting it back in his pocket with care. "And what shall we do for twenty minutes? Perhaps you would like some milk, and a biscuit, while you tell me how you know about the rainbow." He went to his own door and spoke to someone inside. Then he came back and said, "Sit by the window, and tell me how your brother found out."

Marija explained that Berno did not know anything about the rainbow. He had not thought about it at all. While she told Professor Fendor about it a maid brought in two cups of milk and one of coffee, and a plate of biscuits. They ate and drank while they talked.

The professor listened and laughed. " We shall have to look for a fountain that could have cast rainbows," he said. "We still shall not know. Now it is five to ten. We had better look from the window. Wait while I bring some binoculars."

When he had his binoculars he put them to his eyes and looked at Spolet through them.

"There are people in the square," he said. "Now I see a fire-engine. Now the people are leaving the square, because water is falling on them. There is no rainbow yet." Then he watched without speaking. Then he stood up and opened the window as wide as he could. He took the binoculars from his face and looked without their help.

"Without them I can see it perfectly well," he

said. "There is a rainbow standing in the square
at Spolet. I wonder if that is where freedom began."

Marija and Elena were looking as hard as they
could; but they found it hard to pick out even the
village of Spolet, among the green vineyards and
gardens of the hill-side. Professor Fendor lent them
his binoculars and let them look through. Marija
found them wandering all over the mountains.
Then she found the river and followed it down
until she came to houses. Among the houses she
found the square, and in the square there was a
rainbow, standing in its seven colours. Elena could
not find anything at all, with her own eyes or with
the binoculars.

"Never mind," said the professor. "Never
mind. Marija and I have seen it, and that is enough.
I will think about it, and perhaps I shall write a
book about it. We will make Spolet famous. And
of course, now we know the time of day that
Karistan was born. No one knew that before."

"His mother would know," said Elena. "I was
born just after midnight."

"Karistan was born so long ago that everything
was forgotten," said the professor. "And now I
must thank you for coming, and go back to my
work. If you go now you will be in time for the
tram to the town. Thank you for coming. It has
been very interesting."

Marija and Elena curtseyed again, and went out.

The professor still stood by the window, looking at Spolet through the binoculars.

Elena's father was waiting for them when they got off the tram. "Did you see it?" he asked. "Such a lot of water we sprayed. There were complaints, but I am the head of the brigade, and I took no notice. It was time for a practice. Did you mention my name to the professor?"

"We told him everything," said Marija. "And we curtseyed a great deal. Now we will go and tell Berno. We did not tell him before."

Berno had gone out when Marija came back to the house. She made dinner for him, but he did not come, so she had her own and left his on the table. Then she went to see Elena again. Elena came back to play at Marija's house.

Not long after dinner Berno came back. He had been to see a friend and work with him. He came in and threw all his books on the table, because he had done enough work for the time being. He was just going to sit in a chair and rest for a little while, after telling Marija and Elena to keep quiet for him, when there was a knock at the door.

Berno opened it, and there was a taxi driver. The taxi was down in the street.

"Professor Fendor's compliments," said the man, "and he says would Mr. Firovich and his sister and her friend care to join him in a cup of tea and see something interesting."

"Professor Fendor?" said Berno. "Me? I'm Mr.

Firovich, it'll be me he meant. I saw him yesterday. Marija, I've got to go and see Professor Fendor."

"And the young lady too," said the taxi driver. "Professor Fendor was most particular. Two young ladies, he said."

"Here they are," said Berno. "But I haven't shaved. I'm not ready to see him. But perhaps he won't mind. I've been working all day."

Marija and Elena did not think about being tidy or clean. They were ready to go in a taxi anywhere. Berno thought that Elena ought to go home and say what she was doing. The taxi driver said they must hurry, though. Elena ran all the way home and all the way back. After her came her mother, with a hairbrush.

"No time for that, lady," said the taxi driver, and slammed the taxi door after Elena.

"He must be going to have me," said Berno. "That is why he has sent for me. I have got the job. I can go on being a student, and I shall have some money."

"I wonder what job he will give Elena," said Marija.

"I do not know why he wants you," said Berno. He thought it must be something to do with the fountain, though, when they told him about it. He did not know yet. They had hardly finished telling him when the taxi arrived at the castle. Now there was sunshine coming in at the big porch. They got out into the brightness, and the taxi driver

switched off his engine. The porter came out of his
doorway, and told Berno to go straight up to the
professor's room, quickly. Berno hurried across the
hall and up the stairs, with Marija and Elena after
him. The porter went to chat with the taxi driver.

Professor Fendor was in the waiting-room again.
"Firovich," he said. "Marija, Elena. Please come
in and sit by the window again. I have something
else to show you. First, though, a little tea."

The tea was already poured, and there were
chairs by the window. Marija and Elena curtseyed
again, but Professor Fendor stopped them. "We
are friends now," he said. "You need not curtsey
to me again. Now, Firovich, your sister will have
told you about the rainbow in Spolet."

"She was telling me on the way here, sir," said
Berno. He did not want to hear about rainbows.
He wanted the professor to speak straight out and
say there was a job for him. The professor said
nothing about jobs. He had something different
to talk about. He said that he had been thinking
about the fountain in Spolet that they had shown
him that morning. He thought that there could be
a rainbow in Naznir in the afternoon. So he had
telephoned the fire-brigade at Naznir, and at three
o'clock they were going to make a fountain there,
and see whether there would be a rainbow in that
too.

"It depends how the sun lies," he said. "It
should be right at three o'clock."

"I hope it is not," said Marija. "Spolet is where freedom began."

"We do not *know*," said the professor. "We must *know* before we can speak."

"My father will be very sad about it," said Elena. "It was his fire-brigade this morning."

"Truth is important," said the professor. "Now I think we had better start looking."

There was no word to Berno about his job. There was no mention of it at all. The professor did not know yet, perhaps. He would not speak until he knew there was a job for Berno.

The afternoon was like the morning. The professor looked at Naznir with his binoculars, and said what was happening.

"There are people," he said. "There is water rising. It is getting higher. Now it is like a tree. There is no rainbow yet. Ah, there it is. It is like a fire. There is another rainbow at Naznir. See through the binoculars."

This time Elena saw it, and Marija could see nothing. Berno saw it too. Then he gave the binoculars back to the professor. He badly wanted to ask him about the job, but it did not seem to be the right time.

"We are back where we started from," said Professor Fendor. "I thought it would be so. I knew you would be interested to see it."

"You knew and you spoke," said Marija.

"You learn your lessons well, Marija," said the

professor. "Perhaps you will be a student here one day yourself. And now the taxi is waiting to take you all back to Spolet."

"Poor Spolet," said Marija.

"Poor Spolet," said the professor. Then he was a little surprised because Elena kissed him. "You are not angry with me," he said.

"We are friends, you told us," said Elena.

They went back to the taxi. The driver started the engine, and they went down the hill and through the town and home again.

"It is a strange thing," said Berno. "I wish he had told me about the job. That is what I want to know, not about the rainbow. I do not care if there are rainbows in both places at once."

"It could not be morning and afternoon at the same time," said Marija.

"I wonder," said Berno. "I must go and see Elena's father, and then I may go to Naznir. Perhaps I shall be back late. I will visit our cousins who live there."

Berno was late back, because his aunt and his cousins liked to have visitors. But in the morning he was up early, and woke Marija up early too. He waited for the postman as well, in case there was a letter from Professor Fendor. There was no letter.

"We have to go and see him again," he said.

"I am ready," said Marija. "Shall I get Elena?"

"We shall go at eleven," said Berno. "I could not help getting up early. What shall I do until eleven?"

"Why have we to see him again?" said Marija. "He will be tired of us at the end of the week."

Berno thought about that. "I don't think we shall see him any more after today," he said. "Unless he gives me the job, and then I shall see him every day. But still I have no letter from him. Now I can eat no breakfast."

Elena came at eleven. She was very tidy. Her mother had brushed her hair, the same as she had the morning before. "If the professor sees me well-kept two times out of three, then Mother will not be ashamed," said Elena. "Why are we seeing him again, Berno? Father says there will be more trouble for the fire-brigade today. He is going to send all the complaints to you."

"I will think about them when they come," said Berno. "Now I will take a book on the tram with me, and study."

The porter at the castle had begun to know them well by now. As soon as he saw them he said, "I know you have no appointment. You go up, and I will telephone the professor for you."

"Will he see us?" said Berno.

"He's seen you every day for the past week," said the porter. "Twice a day sometimes, if I remember right. Go on up now. I'll tell him."

The waiting-room was empty today. Berno went straight to the window and looked out of it at Spolet and Naznir. They were both small and

white in the distance, hardly showing among the
green vines and the light rocks of the hills.

Professor Fendor came out to them, and made a
little bow towards them. He thought they might
be just coming to visit him in a friendly way. He
did not want them to do that while he was working
but he was going to tell them kindly and not be
angry by any means.

"Good morning, Firovich," he said. "I am
pleased to see you, of course, and the children."

"We wonder . . ." said Berno. "I wonder if you
would look out the of window again, Professor."

"Certainly," said the professor. "What shall I
look at this time?"

"At Spolet and at Naznir," said Berno. "At both
of them, at quarter past twelve. It is not just yet, perhaps, but we have to come when the tram comes."

Professor Fendor wanted to know what he had
to look at.

"You will see it, sir," said Berno. "If you do not
see it I shall be very sorry indeed." He would not
tell the professor what to look for. It would be an
interesting surprise, he said.

The professor brought his binoculars again, and
looked at both villages. "There is nothing yet," he
said. "But there is still five minutes to go."

Berno did not know what to say during the next
five minutes. He was very embarrassed in case he
was wrong to expect what he did. Then Professor
Fendor began to look harder at the two villages.

"Why, Firovich, it is there again, in Spolet. How can that be? There is a rainbow at the wrong time of day."

"Do not forget Naznir," said Berno.

"Naznir is the same," said the professor. "There is a rainbow there too. Look through the binoculars, Firovich."

They all looked through in turn. This time both Marija and Elena saw the rainbows. They each saw two. There was one in Spolet and one in Naznir.

"I will tell you something," said the professor, when he had had another look himself. "There are not two rainbows, Firovich."

"Oh, sir," said Berno. "I saw them both."

"Not two, but one," said the professor. "How many ends has a rainbow?"

"Two," said Marija. "Both on the ground. But sometimes I have seen a rainbow with only one end on the ground and no other end at all."

"Or only in the clouds," said the professor. "Those are rainbows with one end. This is a rainbow with two ends and no middle. If you could make a fire-brigade fly, and put it up in the air between those two, then we could complete the arch."

"But what do you think, sir?" said Berno.

"Think?" said the professor. "I hardly know what to think. I think that both villages are where freedom began. Who can ever quarrel about that

again? Both villages are equal. It could not be
fairer."

"My mother will be pleased," said Marija.
"She is from Naznir, and we are from Spolet."

"Well, that is that," said the professor. "The
rainbows have stopped now. It would be a good
idea if all four of us went down into the town and
had our lunch together. I will just go and tell my
students that I am going out, and then we shall be
ready. When I come back, Firovich, you will tell
me the explanation of the rainbows."

They walked down the hill to the town. The
trams usually went downhill empty and uphill full.
It is easier to walk down. They walked into the
main street, and to the biggest café, and the
professor chose a table on the pavement.

"Now," he said. "Explain."

Berno had been thinking what to say on his way
down from the castle. Now he explained. Marija
did not understand the explanation, except that it
had to do with the distance up the sky that the sun
was at different times in the day, but the professor
understood it. He nodded all the way through
Berno's explaining. Then he called the waiter and
began to order the meal.

At the end of it all, when he had put a great deal
of money on a plate for the waiter, and said,
"Keep the change," he stood up.

"I have to go back to my students now," he
said. "So I will say good-bye."

Elena went round the table to kiss him again. He bent down and took the kiss on his cheek. Then he felt in his pocket and brought out an envelope. "Firovich," he said, "I said I should write to you. The letter was ready when I came out just now, and I brought it with me. It is my answer." Then he turned round and went away, walking up the hill.

Berno held the envelope, and then he opened it and pulled the letter out and tried to read it upside down. He turned it the other way up.

"Marija," he said. "You did not kiss the professor. Go and do so at once."

"But what about the letter?" said Marija.

"Quick, before he goes," said Berno.

Marija ran after the professor. "I have come to say good-bye," she said. She reached up and kissed the cheek that Elena had not kissed.

"We will meet again," said the professor. "I see that your brother has opened his letter. He is coming to work with me at the castle."

"Oh," said Marija. "That is why he sent me to kiss you. You have given him the job." She thought one kiss was not enough reward, and she gave him another on the other cheek.

"I always give jobs to the students with the prettiest sisters, perhaps," said the professor, patting her on the head. "Or perhaps I give them to the students with the most promising brains."

"Elena is the pretty one," said Marija. "Berno has the brains."

THE REINDEER SLIPPERS

Barbara Willard

THE TWO SUITCASES were out on the beds. Alan
and his mother were packing to go away for Christmas, trying to fit in not only their clothes and
sponge bags but also presents for Uncle Jumbo and
Auntie Sue and Sammy. Sammy was Alan's cousin,
and he and his parents lived in the country. His
father, Alan's Uncle Jumbo, was landlord of a very
old inn beside a road that ran across the forest. As
Alan's mother was a widow and had a job in
London, Alan spent a lot of his holidays with
Sammy. It did not matter that he was a year
younger, for he knew a lot of things that Alan
could not know about, living in London as he did.
Sammy knew very little about London, so the
cousins were useful to one another.

Alan's mother kept putting things into his suitcase and then pulling them out again and trying to fit them in differently.

"Need you take these?" she asked, holding out a pair of slippers. "They take up so much room and anyway they're too small for you."

"They're all right," said Alan. "I must take them."

The slippers were made of reindeer hide. Uncle Stephen, who gave the best presents of anyone, had brought them back from a visit to Lapland, a little more than a year ago. Of course Alan's feet had grown a good deal in that time. He did know the slippers were getting too small for him, but he could not part with them and he would never admit that they were at all uncomfortable.

"Promise you'll be good about them, then," his mother said. "Don't go stuffing Sammy up with a lot of tales about them—you know how it annoys Auntie Sue."

"Okay," said Alan, not looking at her, pushing the slippers back into his suitcase.

There was a kind of magic about the reindeer slippers, but they were not by any means the first magic things Alan had possessed. He had a knack of finding such treasures. When he was very young there had been a mysterious bluish pebble which, at least in his own opinion, could make him invisible. Later, a couple of swan's feathers had had extraordinary powers—he could all but fly down the stairs when he was holding them. Then there was a wonderful double conker that every-body at school tried to get hold of, for such a thing had never been seen—but that was so strongly magic that it made him unchallenged king of conkers all through the autumn term.

None of these things had been as good as the reindeer slippers.

Alan had been in the middle of measles when they came. When, hot and aching, he woke in the night, he put out his hand to touch the slippers of reindeer hide and he thought that a whole reindeer was there beside him. He felt the hard bones of the beast, like a strong framework over which the beautiful skin was fitted. Then he seemed to be riding on the reindeer's back, hanging on hard to the strong thick neck, sheltering behind the great antlers as he was carried many miles over snowy wastes beneath a huge sky sharp with stars. *What is your name?* he had asked the reindeer. *My name is Swiftly*, the creature had replied.

In the morning there were only the reindeer slippers, but night after night Alan and Swiftly rode through deep forests together and across wide plains. As they went, Swiftly would tell Alan of life in the Arctic, of the herds moving darkly over the winter land, of battles when the clash of antlers rang for miles in the ice-bound distances; of the soft-eyed does and their fawns, stepping so lightly that their hoofs barely marked the ground.

It was all exactly as described in the book Uncle Stephen had given Alan at the same time as the slippers.

The box that the slippers had been packed in was kept on the high shelf in Alan's bedroom cupboard. It was a sort of magic museum—the pebble, the swan's feathers, the double conker, now shrivelled and small, were laid inside; and one day, no doubt, the reindeer slippers would find a place there, too.

Alan's various magical experiences had got him into trouble with Sammy's mother. Somehow Auntie Sue could only see Alan's tales of being invisible, flying downstairs, riding Swiftly over the snowy uplands, as a lot of silly fibs. Alan, she claimed, was teaching her Sammy to tell lies. At last Alan promised his mother that he would never speak to Sammy again about Swiftly or anything else of the kind. This promise he had already kept for months, so he hardly needed his mother's warning to "be good" about the reindeer slippers this Christmas.

"The best idea," she said, as she watched him push the slippers back into his case, "would be to let Sammy have them. They'd be just about right for him."

"H'm," was all Alan said.

The inn where Sammy lived with his parents was called *The Forester's Quarry*. This was

because, so some people said, there had been a
quarry close by from which had come the soft-
coloured stone of which the house was built, and
all the useful barns and stables and pig-sties
belonging to it, where Alan and Sammy were able
to play in bad weather. *Where's the quarry now,
then?* Uncle Jumbo would demand. He preferred
the other kind of quarry, meaning something
hunted—there had been wild boar roaming the
forest once, and there were still deer and rabbits
and game birds. He was always promising himself
a new sign for the inn in place of the dull old one
that only had the name painted on it. Uncle Jumbo
wanted a picture; a stag's head or a leaping deer,
perhaps, or a hunter with bow and arrow.

There were not a great many trees in the forest.
There were clumps and thickets of them, but
mostly the forest was made up of rolling stretches
of moorland where heather and gorse and bracken
grew. There the wind swept bleakly in winter.
Alan loved it then, for there was hardly a soul
about. He and Sammy would go out for hours.
Sammy was the best sort of companion at such
times, for young as he was he knew a good deal
about birds and animals. He was a good foresty
boy, they said in the village. In the early dusk of
December there was a mysterious blueness over all
the forest and owls were out by half-past four. In
the depth of the cold night foxes barked. Sometimes two or three deer passed quietly by, but

mostly those were in the more wooded parts two miles or so away.

This Christmas was as good as all the others Alan and his mother had spent with Uncle Jumbo and Auntie Sue. Uncle Stephen drove down on Christmas Day and stayed the night. As usual, his presents were the best. Among them was a huge flat parcel for Uncle Jumbo. It was the new inn sign he had been talking about for so long and it was exactly what Uncle Jumbo wanted.

"The fitting screws still haven't come," Uncle Stephen explained. "They should arrive in the post any time. But I suppose if you wanted to you could always use the old ones."

On Boxing Day the sky was black from early morning and anyone could see there was snow on the way. In the middle of the afternoon, Uncle Stephen decided he had better get back to London. Because she had to be at her job next day, Alan's mother went with him. As Alan and the others waved good-bye, the first careless flakes of snow were idly spinning through the dusk.

Alan hardly knew how to wait until the morning. He had never seen the forest covered with snow. When he went to bed he put the reindeer slippers close beside him. In the darkness he put out his hand and felt the fine tough hide. Then he laughed to himself in a rather shamefaced way. Did he still expect the slippers to turn into a full-grown reindeer? Did he still think Swiftly might come to carry him over the snow? He was growing out of the reindeer slippers, so wasn't he perhaps growing out of Swiftly, too?

All night the snow fell. Next morning a grey swollen sky hung low over the stretches of forest. There was lots more snow to come but already everything was changed. Whole bushes had disappeared. The lower branches of the trees, bowed down under their load, had then been trapped and frozen to the ground. No bird was seen or heard. Up in the village the road was silent, for nothing on wheels could enter from any of the side-roads. Soon a wind came howling out of the grey sky and the snow started to fall again, this time mounding up against hedges and walls, doors and even windows. By next morning it took shovels and spades to clear a pathway enough to leave the house.

Then the sky cleared, the sun shone. The snow, hard underneath, dry as powder on top, began to sparkle. Alan and Sammy went out in gumboots and thick gloves. They shouted and yelled in their excitement and their faces tingled with the sharpness of the air, their cheeks and noses turned red.

"Suppose we had a toboggan," Alan said.

"Make one," said Sammy.

All that afternoon they hunted about for something to make a toboggan. It was getting dark, a strange snowy dark like silver, when suddenly Alan saw hanging high up on the wall of the barn where the cars were kept the very thing they had been looking for.

"It *is* a toboggan, Sammy."

Between them they hauled it down. The seats needed a bit of repairing, but that was all.

"I've never noticed it up there in the dark," Sammy said.

When they had fixed the seats, they hid the toboggan behind bales of straw in the corner of the biggest barn. Then they went indoors and said nothing to a soul about what they had found.

Half a dozen times in the night Alan woke and heard the frost humming in the telephone wires. The reindeer slippers were close to his hand. Was it really too late for Swiftly to come and run beside the toboggan? Magic seemed easy because the whole world was under a spell. If there was indeed no Swiftly at such a time, then he would know he had gone for good. Then he would give the reindeer slippers to Sammy.

The night's frost had bound the snow as hard as cement. Where the snow had melted in yesterday's sunshine, dripping down the branches, there was now a film of ice. The glittering twigs tinkled when the wind blew them.

The two boys kept trying to escape with the toboggan, but there were jobs to be done. The snow meant that ordinary things were difficult and everyone was needing help. There was shopping to be fetched from the village, snow to be swept or shovelled, post to be collected because the van could not get round.

"Ask if there's a small parcel," Uncle Jumbo told the boys. "I could get the new sign up if only I'd got the fittings."

"Use the old ones as Stephen suggested," Auntie Sue said.

But for the toboggan, Alan would have wanted to help with the hanging of the new sign. The afternoon came and they had still not pulled the toboggan from its hiding place. Then without warning Alan heard Sammy shouting, "Now! Now!" He went pelting off to the barn without waiting for Alan to reply. Alan followed, snatching his duffle coat from behind the door and pulling it on as he went. He looked wildly around for his boots, but Auntie Sue must have been tidying up again. There was no time to search. It was already after three. As soon as they were out of sight of home they were facing down a long shallow hillside and here they decided to give the toboggan its first run.

"I'll sit in front," Alan said. "You hang on to my middle." He sounded breathless.

"You've got your slippers on!" Sammy cried.

"They're my reindeer slippers, stupid."

"You'll get soaked! You'll die of frostbite!"

"Oh, do get on and shut up! What's the good of a reindeer if its skin can't keep out the snow?"

At first it seemed as though the toboggan was

not going to work. Then it began to move, slithering, slipping sideways, then settling to a straight course as it gathered speed. Suddenly the slope took it and pulled it, and at last Alan and Sammy were rushing over the snow, down the slope towards the hollow, shouting with excitement. Sammy yelled wordlessly, but Alan heard himself crying, "Swiftly! Swiftly!" in a loud excited voice. The toboggan was certainly not Swiftly, but it brought back some of his most magical memories and he felt wildly happy.

The snow was soft in the hollow. They ploughed into it, sending up clouds of white powder, the toboggan's runners making a sound that was almost a squeak on the white surface, as a skate squeaks on ice. For a moment they thought they would spill, but Alan tugged at the rope as at a rein and the toboggan pulled to a gentle stop without unseating them.

Now they were both enchanted. They dragged the toboggan up steep and steeper tracks. Soon Alan discovered how to make it swoop and swerve. It skimmed the snow, avoiding the sudden drifts against hidden bushes and humps of heather, leaping gullies that could have caught its nose and hurled them into a somersault.

The sun had vanished long ago, but the endless whiteness of the ground for miles kept the forest light and it was a surprise when a few flakes of snow came down on all the rest. The boys had been too busy to notice that the darkness in the sky was not night but clouds.

"Come on. Home," said Alan.

"One more!" Sammy cried. "If we go up there we're near a short cut home."

They toiled up as Sammy directed. When they reached the top they were looking over a part of the forest Alan had never seen before. It was not only the snow that made this seem unfamiliar territory. Dotted about the forest were various cottages and farms, lonely and cut off, with only well water for their supply and no electric light. But here there were no roofs at all, only the open rolling plain, empty and mysterious.

"Where are we, Sammy?"

"I told you. Down to the bottom and then there's a short cut."

"But that's in the wrong direction. We go back that way," Alan said, turning and pointing.

"I tell you it's a short cut. I should know. Who lives here—me or you?"

"All right—if you're sure. Hop on. Buck up."

The toboggan shot off once more. But now neither of the boys shouted. They made the down-hill run in silence, Sammy a bit sulky, Alan worried. The snow that had started to fall was very slight, but now the sky did indeed seem to grow darker every minute.

Things Alan had been too much occupied to notice now became horribly obvious—that his feet

were soaked and numb—that back at home Auntie
Sue would be getting worried and Uncle Jumbo
would be getting furious—that Sammy was the
young one and should not have been allowed to
come so far. And that no one knew where they
had gone.

"Which way now, then?" he demanded, when
they reached the bottom of the run.

"This way," said Sammy positively.

He plodded ahead and Alan followed dragging
the toboggan. Now his legs were soaked, as well as
his feet. The snow was deeper here—it was over the
top of Sammy's boots. The heads of low bushes
broke the surface of the snow like swimmers in a
choppy sea. The smoothness all around was criss-
crossed with tiny tracks where mice had run out
from shelter, searched desperately for food, then
scuttled for home. By the edge of a frozen pond
birds of all sizes had come and gone, frantic for
water, patterning the snow with their delicate
prints. A fox had come to the pond, too, and
rabbits—Sammy knew all about such things and
even now he stopped to look at the tracks and tell
Alan which was which. Further on there was a
patch where the snow was flattened and scattered,
and there were some drops of blood and a few
feathers.

"Fox caught a pheasant," Sammy said.

All these things made the forest seem wilder and
lonelier than ever, given up to animals and birds,

with no time or place for boys who had been silly enough to come so far from home.

Sammy was first at the top of the slope. He stood quite still with his back turned. The newly falling snow had given his red woolly cap a white top. Quite suddenly, in that expanse of snow and sky, he looked a very little boy, much more than a year younger than Alan. He needed to be looked after, taken care of, rescued from danger.

"It looks different today," he said in a small voice, as Alan came up with him. He sat down on the toboggan. He was trying hard not to cry. "I thought I knew the way."

"Oh, we can't be far from home," Alan said jauntily. "I wish Swiftly was here. He'd take us."

They had not spoken about Swiftly since Alan made his promise, but for all that, Sammy remembered.

"But he's only a pretend reindeer, Alan. Isn't he? Mum says he's just a lot of imagination."

Alan looked about him. He had so often seen Swiftly in the past, had spoken to him so confidently. What had once been so easy was now quite impossible. He knew that the huge proud antlers he had seen were only dead upstanding branches; he knew that everything Swiftly had told him about his home in the Arctic was what he remembered from books. He was too old; the magic had gone. But Sammy was younger—surely

Swiftly was just the thing to help Sammy now.

"Come on," he said. "You'll freeze if you sit there. We'll leave the toboggan and fetch it another day. Oh, do come on. Swiftly may be waiting just ahead. He often shelters where there are trees. Look! There's a clump of gorse and stuff ahead. The quicker we get to it, the quicker we'll be home."

He pulled Sammy to his feet and began to hurry him along, hanging on to his hand.

Swiftly was not at the next clump of bushes, nor at the next. By the time they reached the third clump Sammy was dragging behind, the snow was falling much faster and Alan could not pretend any longer that he was not afraid. What if they were really lost? The forest was so big. You could go for a comfortable walk of a mile or two, or what Uncle Jumbo called a real walk of ten, fifteen, twenty miles. What if they were on a real walk now?

"There are some trees, Sammy—look, I can just see them. Beside the track. Perhaps Swiftly likes trees better than just bushes."

"Don't you *know* if he does?" Sammy cried, bitter and disbelieving.

They reached the clump of trees. Snow whirled, not in big flakes but in little hard balls that blew over the white ground until it found a mound or ledge to stop it. It was difficult to see, but the

trees seemed to offer some hope. They ringed a
clump of snow-covered gorse, and here was another
small frozen pond.

"He isn't here either," Sammy said. "Mum was
right. Swiftly's just a made-up story. He's not a
reindeer at all."

Alan did not answer. His throat felt hot and
tight. He did not know what to do next. Around
him he saw the tracks of animals that had come to
drink, and found the pond frozen—the same little
mouse scratchings and bird patterns that Sammy
had pointed out cheerfully enough earlier in the
day. There were bigger tracks here, too; sharp,
deep tracks that Alan recognized instantly.

He shook Sammy. "Look here, then! What did
I tell you? Swiftly's been here! Here are his hoof
marks!"

Sammy looked at the tracks and then at Alan.
He gave a wobbly smile and sniffed hard.

"Are you *sure* it's him?"

"He's got tired of waiting for us and gone on,"
said Alan. "Quick! We've got to catch him up.
It's easy to see the way he went."

The deep slots made by the deer's sharp hoofs
led steadily onwards from the bushes up a steepish
hill, like a chain of many links that might be
dragging the boys to safety. In his eagerness Alan
began to go faster, tugging poor Sammy along. He
heard him crying out, but it was only when he fell
flat that Alan allowed a halt.

He stooped beside the younger boy, trying to help him up.

"I can't," sobbed Sammy. "I can't—I can't. . . ."

Alan looked round him in terror. There seemed to be nothing but snow now; snow on the ground, snow in the air and in the sky, so that he hardly knew whether they had been walking or flying. The tracks were beginning to blur. He peered ahead, wondering how soon they would be lost altogether.

He saw something then that made his heart thump. He remembered all the stories he had ever read about people in deserts, people lost on moor and marshland—gazing ahead and thinking they saw what they most wanted to see. . . .

"Sammy . . . Can you see something. . . .?"

Sammy struggled up, dragging at Alan's hand. He, too, screwed up his eyes. Then he gave a shout.

"It's Swiftly," said Alan. "Isn't it?"

"It's Dad's new sign!" Sammy screeched. "He's got it up and it's lighted! It's a stag's head, look— the light's shining right through the eyes! It's *The Forester's Quarry!* We're home!"

First, there were the scoldings, then the huggings and kissings. Everyone had been desperately worried.

"What a stupid thing to do! Going off like that without telling anyone! You ought to be ashamed

of yourselves. You're too old to behave so
thoughtlessly. You might never have got home
alive."

"Alan told me—" Sammy began. Then he
changed what he had been going to say into, "Alan
saw the tracks of a deer and we followed them, and
they brought us all the way home."

"Yes, there's been an old stag nosing about,"
Uncle Jumbo agreed. "You seem to owe him quite
a lot—I'll see he finds a bit of fodder." He looked
at Alan. "You kept your wits about you. That was
good."

Alan was not sure whether he felt pleased or sad.
He would never forget the sudden sight of that
proud, antlered head shining out over the snow.
For an instant, until he saw that the antlers were
the wrong shape, he had truly believed that it was
Swiftly who had brought them home. . . .

Auntie Sue had the reindeer slippers in her hand.
They were black and slimy with wet, as though
they had been fished up from the bottom of a deep
pond.

"Alan—I thought you were a sensible boy.
Fancy going out into the snow in slippers!"

"Yes, but if I hadn't—" Alan began. And then,
like Sammy, he stopped and said something else
instead. "Will they dry all right?"

"They'll dry. But I doubt if you'll ever be able
to get into them again."

They did dry—magically. The skin shrank back

to the shape and size it had been when the slippers were new. That meant they were a whole year too small for Alan. There was nothing for it—he would have to give them to Sammy.

He waited until he was packing to go home.

"Here you are," he said. "If they fit you, you can have them."

Sammy looked at the slippers. Then he got busy rolling up some string he had found in his pocket.

"Don't you want them?" Alan cried.

"No, thanks. I don't want to be bothered with any old reindeer. We've got proper ones in the forest."

"*Proper* ones—" began Alan hotly. But it was no good trying to explain what he felt about Swiftly for he was not entirely sure himself. Was it Swiftly who had got them home, or was it the old stag nosing for food far from his usual haunts?

He gave the slippers a hard pressure, as though reassuring a friend, then thrust them back into his suitcase. He was relieved. Far better for Swiftly to have an honourable retirement and to join the other worn-out treasures in the magic museum, the shoe box safe on the cupboard shelf at home.

THE SAMPLER

Dorothy Clewes

THE NEW chest of drawers sat comfortably between the two casement windows. It wasn't new in the sense that it had come straight from a shop, but new as far as Sarah was concerned.

"You do really need more room for your clothes," her mother had said—and the chest of drawers that had stood in the attic for so long had been the answer. Cleaned and polished, its brass handles gleaming, it waited now for her to fill it exactly as she wished.

"And I've put a roll of wall-paper on your bed that will do for lining the drawers with," her mother had said.

Patterned paper was so much more fun than

plain white—and when Sarah unrolled it she recognized it at once. It was the same as the one decora-
ting her bedroom walls but the rosebuds were more
freshly pink against the white background which
on Sarah's bedroom wall was now faded to a soft
cream. This was the way it had been when it was
new, Sarah thought. Perhaps the chest of drawers
had looked different, too, when it had been new,
its wood not so satin smooth, the colour not so
deep.

It was fun lining the drawers, cutting the paper
the right shape to fit, first the two top small
drawers and then the two long ones underneath.
There was room enough to hold other things besides clothes in the bottom drawer. It was deeper
than the others and should have been as empty as
they were. But when Sarah lifted the old lining
paper an envelope stared up at her. It was yellow
with age, and long and narrow—but fat. If it
had been sealed Sarah would have taken it to her
mother at once but the flap was curled back showing a fold of tissue paper. She hesitated only a
moment and then curiosity got the better of any
other thought in her head. She picked up the
envelope and drew out the paper parcel.

The paper wasn't soft like the tissue-paper she
wrapped presents up in, but crisp as if it had dried
up lying folded for so long in the envelope. But
the something inside was soft. A roll of material,
it looked like. Sometimes her mother saved pieces

of silk left over from an extra special party dress
but this was firmer than silk—and stitched all over.
It was a piece of embroidery. Tails of silk of all
colours of the rainbow hung from it in a fringe,
some lengths short, some long. It was a moment
before Sarah realized that she was looking at it on
the wrong side. She turned it over, unfolding it
until it lay flat on the rug she was kneeling
on.

It should have been a picture, but it wasn't. It
was letters. And figures. They ran in long straight
lines of cross-stitches over the sandy-coloured
linen. The alphabet first in capital letters and then
when it came to Z it started all over again in small
letters. Then the figures began, from 1 to 9,
finishing with a round 0. And in between the rows
were little lines of flowers, daisies, forget-me-nots,
buttercups. After that there was a sentence: BE
GOOD, SWEET MAID, AND LET WHO WILL BE CLEVER,
it read. And right at the bottom of the work a
name was embroidered in the same tiny cross-
stitches: SARAH SERAPHINA, Aged 11, 1844.

It was a little startling to see her own name
staring up at her, and her own age, too—but the
date was a hundred and twenty years ago. Sarah
turned it over wonderingly.

"All those untidy ends," a voice said. "I'm
always telling you, the back of a piece of work
should be as neat as the front. It should be difficult
to tell the difference."

"But a knot is so much easier," Sarah said—and if you couldn't tell the back from the front all the letters on the wrong side would read backwards, she thought, but she didn't say so aloud because it was rude to contradict.

"And I do declare, you are only as far as N," the voice said.

Sarah looked down at the piece of embroidery. She was so sure it was finished but now she could see that she was holding a needle in her hand. It was threaded with green silk that she had just pulled through the canvas after making the tiny cross that completed the letter N.

"And you aren't wearing your thimble. You'll wear a hole in your finger end, you see if you don't."

Sarah looked at the second finger on her right hand. It was peppered all over with tiny punctures and was as rough as sand-paper, but the silver thimble that should have sat on the end of her finger like a little hat felt clumsy and made her finger hot.

"Drawing-room hands, that's what young ladies should have. Put it away now. Master Graham has called." The name was spoken with distaste and a disapproving sniff.

Graham lived next door. He was thirteen, two years older than Sarah was, and her friend. If he had called it must mean that something nice was going to happen. All the nicest things that happened to her happened with Graham. She was already at the nursery door, her hand on the knob.

"—but not before we've washed our hands," Nanny Grose checked her, "and brushed our hair."

Such a waste of time. She had been made to wash her hands before she started up the embroidery and she had had her hair brushed until her scalp tingled only an hour ago. Sarah stood impatiently twisting first on one foot and then on the other while Nanny lifted a handful of hair and re-tied the black velvet bow.

"And if you're playing with Master Graham we'd best leave your overall on."

Sarah looked down at the starched and crimped white overall covering a black velvet frock with lace collar and cuffs and wondered why she had expected to see blue jeans and a yellow cardigan.

"And try and behave like a little lady," Nanny Grose's voice followed her racing footsteps down the stairs, "though it will be difficult with *that* young man."

"I'm glad I wasn't born a girl," Graham said as she jumped the last two stairs and landed unsteadily at his side. "Don't do this and don't do that, how do you stand it? I'd run away but you're a girl and so you can't."

"One day I will," Sarah promised him because if Graham thought running away was a good thing that was exactly what she would do.

"Nanny Grose would catch you before you got

to the end of the road," Graham told her. "You haven't got a chance. You'll do as you're told until someone comes along and marries you, and if no one does you'll stay at home doing needlework until you die."

"I won't, I won't," Sarah shouted him down— but deep inside her she had an awful feeling that what he was saying was true. She wasn't even very good at needlework, she had to remind herself, thinking of how long it was taking her to fill the sandy-coloured squares.

"What will you do, then?"

"I don't know," Sarah said, miserably—because there really wasn't very much she could do,"—but I'll think of something before I grow up. What are we going to play at?"

"We're not going to play. I'm building a house in a tree and I need you to hand me up the wood and the nails."

"A house in a tree—?" Sarah's eyes were wide with astonishment. Graham was a great builder of things. There had been the time when he had built a wheeled carriage out of an old tea chest. He had taken the wheels from the platform of a fine rocking-horse he never played with. He had fixed two seats inside and they had gone careering down the slope of his parents' lawn to end up bruised and bleeding on the rockery because he had not thought to fix a brake. One snowy winter he had built a toboggan which had ended in equal disaster:

Sarah had proudly carried the scar on her forehead from that adventure for days. She was only ever allowed to be mate to his master but when the job was completed he always rewarded her patience and worshipping admiration by letting her be the first to try it out.

It was an old spreading beech tree and to reach the first giant branch Graham had fixed up a rope ladder.

"Like on a ship," he explained. "When you're in the house you can pull in the ladder and no one can follow you up."

He scrambled up the swaying rope footholds and sat straddled over the huge branch. "Now heave me up the wood—and the saw—and the nails."

At the end of an hour there was enough floor space to hold them both. "Come on up," Graham called down to Sarah. "You can see for miles."

The rope ladder was much more difficult to climb up than it had seemed watching Graham. It wouldn't stay still and the hard bark of the tree scuffed the toes of her shoes and took the skin off her knuckles, but she wasn't going to let Graham think she couldn't do it. He pulled her up the last few inches, the rope ladder after her—and she was in another world. It was a shadowed, sun-speckled, secret world with surprising glimpses of the very prim Mrs. Webb next door hanging out frilled and beribboned knickers and voluminous petticoats where they couldn't be seen from neighbouring windows. And there was the very pompous man-servant who belonged to Mr. Soames who lived in the house next door to Mrs. Webb, sitting outside the kitchen door—in his shirt-sleeves, nodding over a large tankard.

"I always knew he wasn't as superior as he made out to be," Graham gloated. "What do you bet I couldn't wake him up?" He reached into his trouser pocket.

"Oh, Graham—the catapult." Sarah put a hand over her mouth to stifle her giggles.

Graham put the dried pea in the sling, drew back the elastic to its full stretch and took careful aim. Two gardens away Mr. Soames' manservant leapt into the air with a yelp of astonishment.

So engrossed were they in the antics of Mr. Soames' manservant trying to decide what was attacking him, and from where the attacks were coming, that they never heard the sound of voices approaching across the lawn.

"—and this tree was here long before the house was built," Graham's father's voice boomed. "A fine copper beech. It could shelter an army without your knowing it—"

Sarah jumped, almost as startled as the man-servant, overbalanced, missed her footing on the platform and shot down through the sheltering branches to land in a shower of leaves on Graham's father's best silk topper. Following in her wake, no less startled and too swiftly to use the rope ladder, came Graham.

It was hard to face Nanny Grose with the velvet frock and pinafore torn beyond repair but at least Sarah was only bruised and shaken. Graham had fared much worse. "This time—boarding school," his angry father had pronounced as soon as he had recovered his breath.

Nanny Grose received the news triumphantly. "And not before time. Discipline is what that young man needs."

"But it was going to be such a beautiful tree house," Sarah said sadly.

"Oh—a clever young man, I grant you," Nanny Grose, said, "but wild and not fit to play with young ladies. 'Be good, sweet maid, and let who will be clever.' The quotation will do very well, I think, to stitch into your sampler."

Sarah picked up the sampler with a heavy heart. Graham was going to school and out of her life. He was right, girls didn't have a chance. She would sit stitching at samplers for the rest of her life.

"Sarah Seraphina, Aged 11, 1844." It was finished at last. Sarah made the last cross-stitch and threaded the silk end neatly through the back of the stitch and put the needle away in its case.

"I wondered what had happened to you, you were so quiet," Sarah's mother said from the door.

Startled, Sarah sat back on her heels, her cheeks pinkly flushing.

Her mother looked over her shoulder. "Why—what have you got there?"

Sarah held up the sampler. "It was in the bottom drawer," she said. "It's my name—but it says 1844."

Sarah's mother took it from her. "Well—for heaven's sake, that's your great-great-grandmother's. You were named after her."

"So she did get married."

Sarah's mother looked at her questioningly and then laughed. "Of course she got married, you wouldn't be here if she hadn't. As a matter of fact she was a very remarkable person. Young ladies in those days were supposed to stay at home, help around the house, arrange the flowers, do needle-work. She rebelled. She actually left home to follow another remarkable person whose name you must have heard of: Florence Nightingale."

"She nursed soldiers—in the Crimean War." Sarah was thinking fast. At school, only a few weeks ago, she had had to write an essay about Florence Nightingale. "She was the first real nurse and hospitals are the way they are today because of her."

"That's right," Sarah's mother said. "Soldiers were dying miles away from home in a strange land with no one to care for them properly. Florence Nightingale called for thirty-eight other nurses to go with her out to a place called Scutari. Your great-great-grandmother was one of the thirty-eight."

Thoughts were stirring in Sarah's head, thoughts mixed up with other thoughts. "—and Graham—was—my great-great-grandfather?

Sarah's mother nodded. "It was really very romantic. As children they'd lived next door to each other and had been close friends. ThenGraham was sent to boarding school, the family moved away, and they never met again—until Scutari. Graham was one of the wounded soldiers in the barrack hospital there."

"Didn't she have a mother?" Sarah asked, her mind on that other Sarah.

"Of course she did—but in those days boys and girls didn't see as much of their parents as they do now. Sarah would have had a nanny."

Sarah ran her fingers gently over the tiny stitches of the quotation. She spoke it softly under her breath: *Be good, sweet maid, and let who will be clever.* Aloud she said: "I'm glad she didn't take any notice of the words."

"Oh, but she did," Sarah's mother corrected her. She paused a moment, thinking. "Maybe it was the poem that started her mind working—or have you forgotten how the rest of it goes?"

For a moment Sarah had but now it was coming back to her. She said with excitement in her voice: " 'Do noble deeds, not dream them, all day long.' And she didn't spend the rest of her life doing needlework. I'm so glad."

Sarah's mother laughed. "As far as I know that

was the only piece of needlework she ever did; she was always too busy doing all those noble deeds." She began to fold up the sampler again, smoothing out the yellow, brittle tissue-paper.

"Oh, please—couldn't I have it?" Sarah pleaded. "After all—in a way—it is mine."

"Well—of course. Why not? And it certainly makes no sense to put it back in the drawer again; but it would be a pity for it to get crumpled and soiled. Perhaps we could get it framed and then you can hang it on your wall as a picture."

It would be much more than a picture hanging on her wall, Sarah thought. It would be a kind of secret between herself and that other Sarah Seraphina who had once been the same age as herself.

TEA WITH ELEANOR FARJEON

Rumer Godden

SHE CAME to meet you at her blue front door that let you in beside the bow window that stretched across the sturdy little house front. She would be wearing a comfortable flowered dress, in china blue and white perhaps—"I don't buy clothes. I wear my old ones"—her feet in equally comfortable strap buttoned shoes, her hair gathered up out of the way, her cheeks rosy, though she was so often ill, and her eyes clear behind her spectacles as she beamed at you; "beaming" was the right word for Eleanor Farjeon, a beam that shone and lit you. Unlike most of us, she was not ashamed of showing her feelings and, if the sight of you made her happy, happiness enfolded you. There was never

anyone more reassuring; I once rang her up and
said, timidly because I am timid about disturbing
busy people, "Eleanor, it's Rumer Godden," and
the answer came back at once, "I knew it was
someone I loved." Yet I was a recent "someone,"
just one in the host of Eleanor's friends, more
friends than even she could count; and hundreds,
indeed thousands more she never knew about but
who knew her from her books, and plays, and
poems.

What was it like to go to tea with her? Unique.
Not in the least like going to tea with anyone else;
you had only to turn off the busy Hampstead
street with its traffic of cars, hurrying foot-steps,
the shops and shoppers with their baskets and bags
and perambulators and dogs, and step onto the
cobbles of Perrin's Walk to know you were in a
different world; not a bygone world—Eleanor
Farjeon was as much of nowadays as she was of
once-upon-a-time, and full of zest for life and,
for all the cobbles and the mixture of shape and
colour in the houses, there was nothing of whimsy
about Perrin's Walk; its cobbles and yards had
served their workaday purpose for more than two
hundred years and where it once housed horses,
carriages and coachmen, it now housed people and
cars—there always seemed to be a man washing
down a car, perhaps two or three cars. The houses
were workaday too, particularly Eleanor's at the
end of the Walk.

As with everything to do with Eleanor Farjeon, the house held surprises—and treasures. It had once been a stable and though it had precious things in it now there was still an earthy quality, a home-liness about it.

You came first into a sitting-room which I never seemed properly to see—the first moments were always completely taken up with Eleanor—but there was an impression of cream colour and faded restful blues and mauves: of old china and flowers, and paintings and photographs of actors, musicians, writers—not only friends but family, because Eleanor's grandfather had been a famous actor, her father a novelist and journalist, her two younger brothers writers as well, her eldest brother a musician and well-known teacher of music who taught many great concert players.

I do not know if anyone ever sat in that sitting-room but it always seemed only an ante-room to the real home. You went through the kitchen, a jumble of a kitchen, and climbed up the wooden stairs—though they were boxed in, they were real stable stairs with a rope instead of a bannister rail. They led to what had been the hayloft and was now Eleanor's workroom, and sitting-room, rest-room—sometimes bedroom for a visiting friend—music room and book room. I know *The Little Bookroom* was in quite another place, in fact quite different but it always seemed to me to be contained in that room though of course it was not dusty as *The Little Bookroom* was—Eleanor's devoted women saw to that—it held another kind of dust that she writes of in her foreword to the book: "mottled gold dust of . . . temples and flowers and kings, the curls of ladies, the sighings of poets, the laughter of lads and girls."

The room was not so much like a hay loft as a ship's hull turned upside down, or an ark; it was peculiarly a room for stories, for talking of ideas, and you sat on a low red-seated chair, looking at the notable Album that had belonged to Eleanor's mother and that held letters from Longfellow, Lowell, Jefferson, Hawthorne, or exchanged news of work, writers and poems, while the treelight came through the windows. Eleanor's typewriter was on her desk table; books, letters, manuscripts, projects were all around; the telephone rang often —it might be the B.B.C. or a publisher or an agent or a friend. There was always a steady, busy hum of life but, always, room in it for you.

The house had two gardens, both hidden away; one, behind the house, had a hammock between two apple trees. The hammock collapsed with Eleanor one day and the garden was so hidden that it was some time before anyone heard her cries and came to help; she could not get up by herself. The second garden was much bigger and we came to it through a grassy and sometimes muddy right of way, a sort of passage with a flower bed on one side, a garden shed on the other. A door in a tall

wall opened on to the garden where we walked on
summer afternoons, along the paths under the
copper beech and between cottage flowers—a
cottage garden in the midst of London! And
an orchard! If *The Little Bookroom* seemed to
me to be upstairs, *Martin Pippin in the Apple
Orchard* was in the garden: it was not quite the
one he describes, laid out in neat plots—these were
overgrown, not neat—but there were "double
daisies, red and white and pink, sweet herbs,
lavender and wallflower, fruit trees and, in a sunny
corner, a clump of flowering currant heavy with
bees". Though we were walking in summer and the
book's description was written of spring, it never
seemed to matter—Martin Pippin was still there.
Eleanor was proud of her roses and hollyhocks,
which seemed to love the garden—I have never seen
any finer. Cats loved it too, and there were always
two or three walking, sitting on the paths, sunning
themselves on the walls; like Eleanor, her cat
Benny had a host of friends and all of them were
welcome. "I have brought a hundred and twenty-
seven kittens into the world," she once told
me.

Though Eleanor walked heavily, slowly, with a
stick and leaning on my arm, "I'll soon be eighty-
three, which is awfully surprising," her eyes and
her ears and her mind were as quick as her own
Humming Bird—one of her books I particularly
loved—extraordinarily quick, quicker than those of

most young people. After all, it was she who wrote:

> You can't catch me!
> You can't catch me!
> Run as swift as quicksilver,
> You can't catch me!
>
> If you can catch me you shall have a ball
> That once the daughter of a king let fall;
> It ran down the hill and it rolled on the plain
> And the king's daughter never caught her ball
> again.
>
> And you can't catch me!
> You can't catch me!
> Run as quick as lightning,
> But you can't catch me! . . .

That garden was filled with poetry; over the hum of the traffic, as quiet as the bees, came the sound of children's voices and of bells, London's bells:

> Where are your oranges?
> Where are your lemons?
> Ring again, sing again,
> Bells of St. Clement's . . .

It was a kind of enchantment and I should have liked to linger there but Eleanor would say, as downright as Martin Pippin himself, "We're going into tea. That's flat!"

Tea was in the kitchen, no matter who came. That particular afternoon I had brought one of Eleanor's American publishers—a most important person in her life; most authors would have made a fuss about her, but we sat around the wooden table with Benny on the cooker wailing for his saucer of milk—a golden cat whose full name was Mr. Benignus Malone! "What do you give your cat to eat?" Eleanor had asked me severely, almost on our first meeting. "Not just fish and milk, I hope. A cat needs more than that," and her satisfaction was immense in hearing that my Siamese Simba had rabbit and liver—"And raw meat?" prompted Eleanor—"And raw meat," I said, "as well as fish and milk."

Eleanor's appetite was splendid—she was not ashamed of that either—so that you were encouraged to eat too. There was toast spread with pate, followed by sticky buns spread with home-made jam, followed by raspberries and red currants from the garden which we ate out of blue glass bowls— they looked almost too pretty to eat—the berries I mean—all this with lashings of tea. As we munched and the tea flowed, talk flowed too—there was never any hurry in Eleanor's house—and she always had something unusual to tell. "Yesterday I was interviewed for a paper," she said.

"But you *never* give interviews," her publisher

and I said together, and indeed the thought of a reporter invading Perrin's Walk was unspeakable.

"That's true," said Eleanor, "but you see, this wasn't just a reporter. He was also the editor, printer, distributor, and the owner, of his paper."

"But how?" we said and, "what paper? Who was he?"

"He was twelve years old," said Eleanor—and this is where Richard Peroni comes into the story.

When I met him he did not look in the least like a reporter, or an editor, more an open-air boy: brown haired, blue eyed, big and well set up with healthy cheeks; in fact, more like an explorer, which in a way he was because this venture began when, at Holloway School in London, where he was a pupil, the librarian asked his form to do a project on various great men and Richard was given Benjamin Franklin. Some boys would have read up the facts in the nearest encyclopaedia and been content with that, but Richard went from the local library to the United States Embassy Library, to the Public Records Office and, amongst other things, he discovered that Benjamin Franklin had made a fortune by publishing a series of almanacks called 'Poor Richard's Almanack''.

"Poor Richard's Almanack." When the family were discussing this, Richard's young brother said, "Why don't you also start a paper with the same name?"

The Peronis were evidently a family that did not

only say, "Why don't you?" They went on to do things and now they formed themselves into an editorial council; it was decided that Richard should publish the paper, a modern Hampstead continuation of Poor Richard's Almanack. It was also decided that he should draw ten pounds out of his banking account—"I had earned this," he told Eleanor, "by helping local tradesmen and by washing cars"—and use it to pay the deposit on a duplicator, the balance to be paid in twelve monthly instalments which Richard's father, who was in publishing, guaranteed, and which Richard was to repay from the sale of the Almanack. The paper, it was decided, should cost twopence a copy or sixpence including postage; its format should be two sides of a sheet of foolscap but, in accordance with old tradition, it should be doubled at Christmas to make a bumper Christmas number: it was to come out on the twenty-fifth of each month and the first issue was published on the twenty-fifth of August, Richard's twelfth birthday.

From its first issue, the paper deservedly had good reviews in, among others, the *Hampstead and Highgate Express*, the *Evening Standard*, the *Guardian*, the *Children's Newspaper*, the *Tatler* and the *Daily Express*, deservedly because it was a serious venture which we watched with respect. It ran for two years, twenty-four numbers, a remarkable feat in consistency for so young a boy. "I got thoroughly sick of it at times but I had to pay for

the duplicator," he said with honesty, but it is clear
that Richard also had the kind of obstinacy, the
perseverance teachers are always talking about at
school, that makes for achievement. Later on he
told me he had liked the work of printing his
issues on the duplicator, disliked the selling and
distribution but he did both, and the work brought
its rewards. Richard was invited to a television
studio, to I.T.A., to a tour of a ship in the Port of
London, and had letters from as far away as
America, Rhodesia and South Africa. The success
was enough to make any young editor have feathers
in his cap; but Richard had, one would guess, little
use for feathers and he kept his paper firmly to its
policy which was a modest but interesting one: to
link the past, present and future of Hampstead by
featuring a Hampstead celebrity of the past, a "write
up" of one of the many celebrities living in Hampstead at the present day, and to give the news of any
achievement of a local boy or girl. To seek these
interviews with the "living famous" Richard made
application by letter, typing his letters himself
though his mother cut the stencils of the accounts
of each interview.

He had the happy idea of linking Eleanor
Farjeon in an issue with Kate Greenaway, that
beloved artist for children "whose beautiful
drawings," he wrote, "so fascinated the mothers of
Europe and America that they dressed their children in clothes based on her designs." (He does not

mention her books.) Kate Greenaway had herself issued a series of almanacks—"It all links up," as Eleanor would have said—and had lived in No. 50 Frognal, not far away from Perrin's Walk; this was interesting, but the factor that made Eleanor Farjeon consent to see Richard was, as she told me afterwards, that his efforts reminded her of her father in his early days when, at thirteen, Benjamin Farjeon was apprenticed to a printer. One day, when he was going to work, he saw a book open in a window and stopped to read the pages; he was so fascinated that he came back, day after day, hoping to read more and each day found the page turned by the bookseller, so that he could read on.

Eleanor Farjeon told Richard much about her father but, as well as listening, Richard, like all reporters, had a set of questions ready to put to her:

"I asked her," wrote Richard in his article:

(1) When was your first book published?
(2) If you had not been a writer, what would you have liked to have been?
(3) Which of your works has given you the greatest pleasure?
(4) What are your interests outside of writing?
(5) Who had the greatest influence in your youth upon you as a writer?
(6) What advice would you give to a boy or girl who desires to write books?

"In reply she told me that she had written verses from about nine years of age and a theatre manager, Augustin Daly, had published some on a satin programme of one of his shows. Her first book *Nursery Rhymes of London Town* was published in 1916.

"There was no doubt what she would have liked to have been if she hadn't been a writer as her answer "A cook" was given almost before I had finished the question.

"The work which gave her the most pleasure was *A Nursery in the Nineties* and her interests, outside of writing, are Theatre, Cooking, Cats, Cricket (she follows with great interest the fortunes of Sussex), and Music most of all. Her advice to a boy or girl who wanted to write books is, 'Don't copy anything you have read. Learn to love words.'" Richard went on to write of her family and ended, "Like the bookseller who turned the pages for her father, Miss Farjeon turned the pages of her life for me. I will always remember her generosity."

Eleanor had a way of making you generous too, often bigger than you really were, and more understanding. I once sent her a gift of flowers and, on the same day, she gave them away. I might have felt rebuffed, hurt but, when Eleanor explained, I felt expanded and twice as warmed; she wrote, "A friend came, in great need, and your red roses especially moved him so I gave them to him. He said, 'Oh *no!*' but I said I had had them, fully, the moment they were sent, and he took them. So you see, love shared is love doubled."

"Love shared." Of all the poems Eleanor wrote, perhaps the best loved is the long poem—it makes a book—of "Mrs. Malone," the old woman who, although so poor and neglected, always had room for one more:

> For each she had something
> if little to give,
> "Lord knows, the poor critters
> Must all of 'em live."
> She gave them her sacking,
> Her hood and her shawl,
> Her loaf and her teapot—
> She gave them her all.
> "What with one thing and t'other
> the fambily's grown,
> And there's room fer another,"
> said Mrs. Malone.

"Room for another": for a fledgling reporter, a fellow writer, an American publisher, a sad man who loved red roses, a hundred and twenty-seven kittens; but it was not only tea, or saucers of milk, or stories or memories, or petting that Eleanor Farjeon gave; it was something more, something transcendent that came out of her love so richly shared.

In *Martin Pippin in the Apple Orchard* Eleanor wrote of a river—a strange river in Sussex, Martin Pippin's country and, for years, Eleanor's, but one guesses there is such a river in every country—an exceedingly strange river, at once "the biggest and yet the littlest known, fullest of dangers and hardest to find." Only a few grown people have ever found it, yet it can be found with a child's help, which is perhaps how through her work Eleanor so clearly found it herself. Children play in it. "None but children," says Martin Pippin. "Above all the child which boys and girls are always rediscovering in one another's hearts—even when they have turned grey in other folks' sight." The source of it is a mystery, so beautiful that "after years of gladness and a life kept always young" when anyone discovers it they will never come back again.

Eleanor Farjeon will never come back again; the blue door is shut now, but she is not gone; she will never go as long as there are children—of all ages—to read her books and poems. As for us who had the luck to know her—if we live as Martin Pippin says, "Years of gladness, a life kept always young," perhaps one day we shall join Eleanor again in some celestial tea party, such as only she could conjure, in heaven.